M000033132

Firewood Happens

Firewood Happens

Life, Liberty, and the Pursuit of Happiness
in Minnesota's Northwoods

Mike Lein

Jackpine Writers' Bloc, Inc.
Menahga, Minnesota   56464

Some of the chapters in this book have appeared in edited forms in other publications as noted below.

The Lake Country Journal Magazine: "Outhouse Talk," "Something Old/Something New," "The Chainsaw Conundrum," "Ode to Thumper," "The Ultimate Winter Vehicle," "A Friend Like Kim," "Firewood Happens," "The Ol' Red and White," "Night of the Creeper," "A Morel Moment," "Hunting Colors," "Fresh Fish on Ice."

The Talking Stick: "Movin' On Up," "The Curse of Boat Addiction," "Holding on to Winter," "Labrador Spring," "My Northwoods Persona," "Winter" originally published as "Winter Life."

Cabin Life, Cabin Living Magazine: "Dock Tales," "Deck Time."

Muzzle Blasts Magazine: "Magic Deer."

Fur-Fish-Game Magazine: "Deer the Hard Way."

Northwoods Press: "The Order of the Evening."

All illustrations and cover artwork contributed by Erik Espeland.

©Copyright 2016 Jackpine Writers' Bloc, Inc.
Jackpine Writers' Bloc, Inc., Publisher
13320 149th Ave
Menahga, MN 56464

2016 Mike Lein, All Rights Reserved.
Printed in the United States of America
ISBN #978-1-928690-28-3
First Paperback Edition

Acknowledgments

Several years ago, a fellow member of an Internet-based writers' group commented on some of the stories included in *Firewood Happens*. She also suggested a title. "Call it *Without the Cabin*," she offered. "Because, without the cabin, none of this stuff would have happened." I didn't choose that title, but she was right. Without our simple cabin, most of this book would not have happened. Interesting characters would have gone unknown. Adventures would not have been adventures. Dreams would not have become reality.

So first in this list are all the friends, neighbors, and family that contributed to construction of the cabin and the stories that happened around it. I won't try to name you all; it would take up much too valuable book space and I would miss someone. But without all of you, there would be no stories and no book. THANKS for letting me take advantage of you all. Let's continue the fun!

Chronologically speaking, the next thanks should go to the Listening Point Foundation of Ely, Minnesota. Listening Point Foundation is dedicated to preserving Listening Point and advancing Sigurd Olson's legacy of wilderness education. Listening Point is the cabin Sigurd Olson wrote about in his book of the same name. I rank it as the best cabin book ever. A visit to Listening Point in the fall of 1998 reacquainted me with Sigurd's books and introduced me to the hard-working people of the foundation including Chuck Wick (Vice-President), Alanna Dore (Executive Director), and Robert Olson, son of Sigurd. I left Listening Point inspired to write. Thanks to them for the ongoing inspiration and friendship. Please check out www.listeningpointfoundation.org for more info on the foundation.

Next are the many editors that saw fit to publish, in one form or another, many of the stories in this book.

Jodi Schwen, former editor of *The Lake Country Journal Magazine* in Brainerd, Minnesota, deserves Honorable Mention. She was the first to send me an acceptance notice ("Outhouse Talk"), gave me confidence to keep on writing, and continued publishing my stories. It's nice to be able to claim "Frequent Contributor" status with a first class publication. Other magazine acceptance notices followed. Individual stories included in *Firewood Happens* have appeared in at least eight separate publications. A list is included in the front of the book to ensure they are acknowledged.

A really big thanks to the leaders and members of the Jackpine Writers' Bloc, Inc. of Park Rapids, Minnesota. I tried several writers' groups and Internet classes before I stumbled across this group. I have stumbled no farther. Many members read draft stories, offered constructive comments, and made them something editors wanted to publish. Along the way they got me over the fear of writing dialogue and forced me to write fiction for variety. The Jackpine Writers' Bloc Board of Directors agreed to publish this book. Special thanks to Sharon Harris and her editorial skills, Tarah L. Wolff for editing and formatting, Deb Schlueter for ideas and edits, and Jerry Mevissen for inspiration and lines to occasionally plagiarize.

Finally, Erik Espeland of Field Hands Natural Goods, Landscapes, & Illustrations gets credit for the cover and illustrations. You can find more of his work at www.Field-Hands.com or email him at EspelandArt@gmail.com.

Table of Contents

Firewood Happens

Life, Liberty, and the Pursuit of Happiness
in Minnesota's Northwoods

Prologue

The Cabin at Crooked Lake

Turn left off a dusty country road, just past the four towering white pines. Follow the driveway straight back through the forest, staying left as it forks and wanders up a steep hill. Then take a sharp right at the Labrador Retriever Crossing sign. A log-sided cabin waits ahead with a single red pine standing guard on the left and a grove of mature aspens at the right. Crooked Lake shimmers behind a simple two-story structure. An outhouse tucked discreetly in the woods hints at simple accom-modations. Whatever the season, the cabin is waiting.

Autumn is a battle of furious activity and contrasting colors. The blue jays and the chipmunks compete for the last acorns; the aspens sheltering the cabin turn to pure sunlight gold to combat the crimson maples and the earthy brown oaks. The collage of colors reflected in the still waters of the lake begs for a skilled artist and an easel.

A truly hardy soul can experience the cold of a Minnesota winter night at the outdoor fire pit with the amber light of the campfire reflecting off the cabin and bright stars above in the clearest sky you have ever seen. Northern lights might appear, changing shapes and shifting from iridescent green to hazy purple while the lake booms, pings, and groans with the effort of making more ice. Inside, the wood stove provides homegrown heat with the flames dancing and glowing from hand-split oak behind the glass door.

A spring visit is tonic for the winter weary.

The forest surrounding the cabin teems with life as the dock is rolled into the icy cold water. Gaudy wood ducks check out the nest boxes hung high in the trees and wave after wave of songbirds passes on their northward journey. Back in the swamp, frogs belt out melodies designed to deafen all other courtship songs as the first loons dance and yodel on the lake.

Let's not skip summer. The deck with an empty chair beckons in front of the rust brown siding. A few mosquitoes whine, but the hummingbirds buzzing at the nectar feeder's fake red flowers and the loons wailing from the lake drown them out. The fishing tackle and boats beg to be used. The dogs search for sticks to be thrown. Life must be prioritized.

An empty chair filled. A cold beer opened. An afternoon wasted?

Outhouse Talk

Ever notice that those of us that own lake homes or cabins tend to brag too much in certain situations? Think about it. Snapshots of the cabin have replaced the baby pictures on our smart phones and we're not afraid to show them to strangers. Give me an audience at work or any social engagement and before long our humble cabin looks and sounds like a wilderness paradise complete with sandy beach, towering pines, and fish that are huge, stupid, and easy. The results are predictable. What loose-talking cabin owner hasn't had a new found "friend" or, worse yet, a distant relative threaten to come and visit for a week or so?

Please don't call me anti-social. Spending time with family and friends sharing our good fortune is a huge part of the cabin lifestyle. But let's be honest: if you own a cabin or lake home, you have met these people—the ones that show up with the whole family, burn up all the boat gas, eat and drink everything in sight, and then disappear without even offering to mow the lawn. So what can the typical Minnesota Nice lake cabin owner do to discourage these freeloaders? Here's where I, at least for the time being, have an advantage over the "typical" cabin owner.

Allow me to further elaborate. My spouse Marcie and I have tried to build our cozy little cabin with style and tradition in mind. We have rustic log siding on the outside, locally milled aspen paneling on the inside, and an open air deck for socializing until the beer runs out or the mosquitoes show up. We now have electricity and light at the flip of a switch. Other major investments, including a well and septic system, will have to wait until both of our sons have put college behind them and a few of those bills are paid.

In the meantime, an old-fashioned outhouse (made politically correct and non-polluting by means of a sealed tank), serves several purposes. There's the obvious—no need for details or discussion. Less obvious is the role of unwanted visitor repellent. If I find myself talking too much and sense one of these unsavory characters is getting too interested, I make sure to mention the lack of indoor plumbing. This usually sends them running—or at least politely dropping out of the conversation and exiting my immediate area.

Most of the time, the mere mention of an outhouse works. Fewer and fewer people have one of these in their past to wax nostalgic about. Still fewer seem willing to revisit "the good old days" with a long walk in the dark of night. However, these potential pests can be persistent. This might require that I ramp up the outhouse talk and take it to a "higher" level. I might break out the ever popular, and unfortunately true, story of the hornet's nest in the outhouse. I don't get overly descriptive just yet. I've found it's better to let the listener's imagination run wild with their own scenarios.

If this doesn't faze them, I add a bear to the outhouse stories and pile on the details to hurry the process along. Early on in our cabin days, I made the mistake of storing the bird/chipmunk seed in the outhouse. A bear wandered out of the dark depths of thousands of acres of state forest and investigated.

Fortunately, the outhouse was not occupied at that particular moment.

The deep claw marks etched into the weathered plywood door tell a story of initial frustration. The beast must have then remembered that it was a big strong bear. It hooked its claws under the door, ripped it off the hinges, tossed out life jackets, canoe paddles, fishing rods, and tools, and helped itself to most of fifty pounds of sunflower seed. The bruin then proceeded to use the outhouse for its intended purpose. Sadly, I assume that it must have been a male. His aim was bad and he failed to lift the seat.

So what happens when all these scare tactics don't work? Then it's time to admit that I might have misjudged this person's character. If they are willing to subject themselves to cold and darkness, hornets and bears, perhaps they may be suitable company at my lake country paradise. Then they too will gain experience that can be used to stimulate conversation at social engagements. They will have bravely taken the outhouse walk. They can now talk the outhouse talk.

Something Old,
Something New

The big round dial of the thermometer read twenty degrees below zero when the January sun rose outside the unheated camping trailer. The dog and I had survived the night in relative warmth—her with an extra blanket and genuine fur coat, and me snuggled inside two sleeping bags with a wool stocking cap pulled down over my ears. A hectic day of work on the unfinished cabin waits for us. First we need to head into town to treat ourselves with a hot breakfast. That sounds like a simple plan, except we had driven the almost-new family SUV this weekend instead of the trusty old truck. It must have been engineered to climb warm mountains. It won't start.

No problem, we'll move on to Plan B. Just get out the generator, fire it up, make some home-made electricity, and perform a little electro-shock therapy on the vehicle's battery. However, the new electronic ignition, brand name, latest-thing-in-backup-power won't start either. It barely turns over with a crankcase full of oil turned thick as molasses by the bitter cold.

Time for Plan C. Strike a match, light the old-fashioned, low-tech, kerosene heaters, place the generator between them, bake it until it starts, jumpstart the dead SUV, and go have breakfast. Luckily that plan comes together several hours later. Ripley the Retriever and I four-wheel out of the unplowed driveway, with the heater blowing full blast, still hungry, cold, and ready for a hot meal. Let's call it "brunch" instead of breakfast now.

Ever notice how the latest and greatest in

equipment/tools/gadgets don't always live up to their advertised claims? Or conversely, how old-fashioned, low-tech, outdated stuff still is useful around the cabin or home? Equipment manufacturers and the young and untested may disagree, but I have plenty of hands-on experience and proof.

Take the genuine Swiss army knife always in the leather sheath on my hip, purchased over twenty years ago in downtown Zurich, Switzerland. It's not as elaborate as the stainless steel multi-tools that are all the rage with fashionable sportsmen. Yet it's smaller, lighter, and manages to perform just about any task from cutting a rope to opening a bottle of wine. I live in absolute fear of losing this handy little knife since many others have disappeared over the years of hunting, fishing, and roaming around.

And how about the old green gas lantern, hanging from the new rafters of the cabin? Marcie and I bought it over thirty years ago as a critical part of a complete camping outfit. It has illuminated many a campsite picnic table, hissed away over late-night fish cleaning, heated the portable fish house, and provided light for cabin work long after sunset. It never requires batteries or a weird light bulb that's impossible to find. A little gas and an occasional new mantle are all it ever asks.

I have plenty of other examples, like my sturdy old aluminum canoe that can bounce off a rock and keep on floating without needing a trip to the repair factory, but the prime example is the outhouse tucked away by the big white oaks. I look forward to the day when the cabin has indoor plumbing complete with sink, shower, and flushing toilet. In the meantime, the outhouse does have advantages.

There's no need to perform the tedious fall ritual of draining pipes to close the cabin for the winter. We simply lock the door and walk away worry-free. Frozen septic tank and drain field? Not a problem for us. The outhouse freezes up but it just doesn't matter. It's ready when you are.

This is not to say that an outhouse or other seasoned equipment can't be improved. Sometimes the marriage of something old with something new is a good thing. Unlike the outhouses on the old farmsteads I grew up on, this one has a sealed watertight tank to deal with modern environmental regulations and the real worries of well and lake contamination. And our outhouse does have a truly modern convenience that we never had on the farm: an insulated toilet seat.

A local artisan handcrafts this unique invention that I recommend to any cabin dweller who must deal with a frigid outhouse. It's cleverly made from recycled foam insulation and scrap wood paneling. It needs no batteries, electrical cord, or fuel, and conveniently hangs on a nail when not in use. And it never ceases to function in cold weather. Simply place it over the hole, take a seat, and enjoy instant warmth. All our cold weather friends sing the praises of this invention and the forward-thinking, talented craftsman who engineered it.

Thus I would argue that experience and maturity are important attributes in the cold northwoods, whether you are man or machine. Especially in the outhouse. Go ahead and try the new, high-tech, molded plastic seat if you disagree. Just make sure your truck will start first. We might have to make an emergency trip to town to treat a very delicate case of frostbite.

The Chainsaw Conundrum

When a tree falls in the forest, it may or may not make a sound. However, cabin owners know what will happen. The tree will block the driveway, crush the newest vehicle in the yard, or maybe even come to rest on the roof of the cabin. Immediate action must be taken. No, not a call for help or a report to the insurance company. Instead the typical male cabin owner will uncase his prized chainsaw in anticipation of playing Northwoods Hero. That's when the real problems start.

While the chainsaw may be one of the most vital and versatile power tools in the cabin owner's arsenal, it's also the most cursed and the most cursed at. The starter cord will be pulled. And pulled. And pulled again. Even the strongest Paul Bunyan Wannabe will resort to profanity.

This situation occurs with such frequency that it deserves a proper title. I believe "The Chainsaw Conundrum" appropriately sums up the gravity and complexity of this challenge of life in the woods. Given my lack of mechanical ability and my genetic tendency towards Scandinavian frugality, my personal struggles with the chainsaw conundrum have been many, including a classic recent affair.

A call for help came early on a summer morning. A nasty overnight storm had passed through a friend's farm. I loaded gear into the truck and headed over to lend a hand. Downed trees were partially sawed and hastily stacked around the farm yard by the time I arrived. The owners and closer neighbors had already taken care of high priority work and moved on to help others, leaving minor issues to be dealt with later. I contemplated tackling the oak limb laying across the still intact roof of the chicken coop. Good judgment prevailed for once. Climbing around on a roof with a chainsaw, by myself, somehow seemed like a bad idea.

I chose instead to bump the truck down a field road to check the woods for blocked trails and damaged deer stands. An exploratory walk confirmed that several once mighty oaks, and many lesser aspen and birch, had succumbed to the storm. Worst of all, one favorite deer stand, "The Freeway," was now nothing more than a mangled heap of branches and weathered wood. No time to grieve; there was chainsaw work to be done.

I walked back to the truck and pulled out my almost-new saw, recently purchased on sale at a major department store. It started with only a couple of pulls and I began turning a storm-blown birch into firewood for the farm's owners. My good fortune was short lived. The saw sputtered and died without making enough wood for a decent campfire. It stayed dead despite many pulls on the cord, threats, and questions about the manufacturer's ancestry.

In this case, there was a backup plan. I bumped back down the trail and up the gravel road to the nearest neighbor. Kenny wasn't home, but his power tools were and I knew where he kept them. I was back in action in no time with a better saw than my own lifeless hunk of metal and plastic. That's what friends and neighbors are for.

This example clearly illustrates a major facet of the chainsaw conundrum. While there is no way to avoid all chainsaw problems, the surest way to have a working chainsaw in an emergency is to own several high quality saws. The best, and therefore the most expensive chainsaws, do have fewer problems. I stress fewer, having seen a grown man near tears when his imported Swedish chainsaw refused to start, in a critical situation, with witnesses present.

These saws typically cost about half a house payment. Thus owning even one is beyond the means of many, myself included. We are therefore driven to purchase several cheap saws with the hope that at least one will work when needed. The trouble with this plan is that the frustration a chainsaw causes the owner is inversely proportional to the price of purchase. For the mathematically challenged, this means that the less you pay for a saw, the more frustration it will cause.

Cheap chainsaws do come with guarantees. They are guaranteed to be difficult to start, hard to adjust, and expensive to repair. This guarantees many chainsaw problems with several problem chainsaws. Or, forgive me, a self-perpetuating chain of saw problems.

An obvious compromise would be to own one expensive, dependable saw and a cheaper, less dependable one for backup. In practice, this only further confounds the conundrum. Which saw should be used first on a critical project? It would be hard to question a decision to start with the best saw and save the cheap saw for backup. But think this through. Can the cheap saw be counted on when the chips quit flying? Will it start when the "good" saw is stuck in a tree teetering over the cabin? Perhaps using the cheap saw first and using the good one for backup is worthy of consideration.

Another solution would be to borrow a backup saw from a friend or neighbor, just in case. I have succumbed to this solution several times. As logical as it may sound, this strategy should be used with all due caution and with full knowledge of consequences.

All chainsaws, especially cheap ones, come with

personal quirks. No two are alike. The borrower is not apt to know a particular saw needs to have the primer bulb pumped three times, the starter rope pulled twice, the bulb pumped twice more, and then pulled again before it will start. Then there's the question of repairs. Given the shortage of good small engine mechanics who work cheap, repairing a neighbor's broken chainsaw may cost more than the original purchase price. The likelihood of a breakdown while you are using it or, worse yet, the next time the owner uses it, is high. This will lead to your name being taken in vain along with the chainsaw.

Finally, the chainsaw conundrum is often complicated by operator error. When I returned home after my earlier example, I enlisted the help of a good friend to diagnose the dead saw. Neil, a fulltime farmer and an experienced mechanic, suggested draining the gas and starting over with fresh fuel. I spun the cap off the gas tank and tipped the saw to drain the contents.

This turned out to be impossible since it was completely empty. With Neil watching and laughing quite hard, I filled the tank. The saw started on the first pull. I said nothing. There was nothing much to say. You can't blame the chainsaw, or the chainsaw conundrum, if you're out of gas.

Ode to Thumper

I subscribe to an environmentally friendly low maintenance lawn care philosophy at the cabin, especially near the lakeshore. I don't think the suburban landscaped look fits with natural northwoods décor. The last thing I want to be reminded of while relaxing at the lake is the green, green grass of home. That said, it is necessary to knock down the mosquito habitat, trim back the poison ivy, and mow trails to the neighbors' campfire rings once in a while. Not just any mower will do for this job. One needs a mower like Thumper, a genuine cabin lawnmower.

True cabin lawnmowers are rarely less than a decade old. More often they're of legal age. Some may even qualify for AARP membership. Most have brand names that are no longer recognizable or legible due to rust, oil leaks, and paint loss. They require ear protection to operate, do double duty as bug foggers, and refuse to start within a half hour of the first attempt. Real cabin lawnmowers never have electric start—at least that works. Most are acquired at garage sales or come free from friends or relatives that can no longer stand their quirks. They all have quirks.

Thumper met most of these criteria. It started life as a shiny red Sears Craftsman sometime back in the '80s. Mowing vacant lots for baseball fields soon led to premature aging. The most obvious symptom was a tooth-jarring, thumping vibration caused by a badly bent crankshaft. Some people would have given up on Thumper. Those people didn't have need for a cabin lawnmower.

I moved Thumper to our lake lot and used it to keep the forest at bay while we planned the cabin. Being stored under a tarp, grinding down tree stumps, and flinging rocks increased the thumping and created new quirks. The handles couldn't stand the strain of northwoods mowing. They kept breaking off and I kept cutting out the breaks and bolting the handles back on, shorter each time.

Next the throttle cable broke, creating the need to manually adjust the speed with a little lever on the back of the motor. Then Thumper decided it didn't like moisture. Try to start it after a good rain and one had better know how to drain the carburetor bowl without losing the drain plug in the grass. It only took a couple of years to end up with a vibrating, difficult-to-start, hard-to-adjust mower with handles the right height for a leprechaun.

Eventually these maladies overcame Thumper. Sad as it was, the time came to make that final trip to the County Recycling Shed and begin the search for a replacement. I struck pay dirt (or so I thought) when neighbor Tom acquired two well-used mowers and offered to share. What could be better? A rider to cruise the nine-hundred-foot driveway and a self-propelled walker to trim around trees. All I had to provide was a little gas and maybe a beer or two around the campfire.

However, these cabin mowers came complete with their own personalities. The rider didn't have electric start. You had to yank the starter rope from behind while remembering to have the mower deck up and the drive belt engaged. Or was it with the mower deck down and the drive belt disengaged? Failure to follow the correct procedure resulted in the belt popping off. That meant easy pickings for the mosquitoes and deer flies while I fumbled to replace the belt, sprawled in the dirt under the mower. And I could never remember if the key was actually "on" when it was in the "on" position, or what direction the fuel shut-off valve had to point.

The push mower was a similar head case. The

engineer that designed this monstrosity must have won a contest for adding the most levers, handles, and switches to one lawnmower. After a while, I came to the conclusion that Tom only offered to share these mowers so that he could secretly get humorous footage on his camcorder.

I longed for my good old Thumper and started weighing options for a cabin lawnmower to call my own. A new mower didn't seem a practical solution since a bent crankshaft or similar condition was a foregone conclusion. My dilemma solved itself when Marcie's father offered up his old Lawn Boy for ten bucks at a garage sale. It seems that it had become too hard for him to start due to several age-induced issues. I snapped it up and trucked it north to the cabin.

The true test of this new lawnmower came when brother-in-law Darv graciously offered to mow the lawn while I handled other chores. "Sure," I replied, trying to keep a straight face. "It's right next to the outhouse."

I could have mentioned the lawnmower's quirks, like the short starter rope, the sensitive safety shutoff switch, and the cracked fuel primer bulb. But that wouldn't have been much of an experiment or much fun. I disappeared around the corner of the cabin to monitor the experiment in relative secrecy. Five minutes later, he was still pulling the too short rope while inventing imaginative new words. Somewhere in that great lawnmower junkyard in the sky, I'm sure Thumper was smiling.

The Ultimate
Winter Vehicle

As yet another Minnesota winter bears down on us, those of us that live and/or recreate in the North Country know it's time to decide what vehicle to drive for the next six, seven, or eight months. The family van got us through all the travels and errands of summer, but it's not going to do the job when school closings start blaring from the radio and snowdrifts block the road to the deer shack or the cabin. We're going to need a real winter vehicle—a four-wheel drive that will start at forty below and is tough enough to withstand being pulled from the ditch multiple times.

This isn't a decision to be made lightly. In fact, I recently found out that I still had a thing or two to learn despite over forty years of experience in dealing with winter and vehicles.

Given my Scandinavian frugality, my winter vehicle at the time was a battle-worn old pickup. My trusted independent mechanic informed me that it had a terminal case of bad valve lifters. The engine was an oddball that would require a valve job costing double what the rusty fourteen-year-old truck was worth. "Drive it 'til it dies, push it into the road ditch, take the license plate off, and walk away," Mick advised.

Not being that type of guy, and not wanting to be stranded in a howling blizzard when it happened, I started the frustrating exercise of shopping for a replacement while the old truck still was mobile. Most advertised used trucks were older, newer, bigger, smaller, or more abused than my idea of a replacement. They all were overpriced. I had almost given up hope when I stumbled across an eight-year-old Sport Utility Vehicle with only 70,000 miles on it. It looked good— the salesman said it had been driven by an elderly lady.

The SUV seemed to have advantages over a truck. It had four doors, seating for five, luxurious options, and a high-tech dashboard with digital gauges that made me feel like I was flying a spaceship. It even looked good enough that Marcie and our sons might not be embarrassed to be seen in it. It could be a multi-purpose vehicle for family trips to the cabin, and hunting and fishing expeditions with the guys and dogs.

After a bit of hard bargaining and despite the "as is" sale terms, I drove away with shift-on-the-fly four-wheel drive, genuine leather seating, air, cruise, power "everything," and even a CD player. I was so enamored with the shiny red SUV that I made plans to customize it one paycheck at a time, adding options like a chrome "deer catcher" grill guard, big tires, heavy-duty suspension, and a custom exhaust for better mileage and a cool rumble. I wouldn't have just a winter vehicle. I would be blasting through drifts with "The Ultimate Winter Vehicle!"

First, a few minor issues like a bad temperature sensor needed to be dealt with. I had Mick charge up the air-conditioner while he was at it. Then the CD player broke. That was an easy fix. My youngest son is an electrical whiz. He upgraded it to a six-disc player complete with remote control.

I was ready to add more fun stuff when Marcie happened to lift up a floor mat. "What's this green goo on the carpet?" she asked. I knew what it was. So did Mick. $450 and a new heater core solved the antifreeze-soaked carpet problem. Writing Mick the check for that repair was painful. You do need a heater core in a winter vehicle.

It wasn't the last check I wrote Mick. Within a year, the transmission quit transmitting, the brakes broke, and the turn signal thingie stopped signaling. Then its shiny red dead carcass needed to be towed from the cabin's yard at thirty below zero to replace the starter, battery, and alternator. Next were tires, struts, and an exhaust system. Forget the big fat tires, the off-road suspension, and the high-performance exhaust. "Just give me the cheap stuff, please," I begged the mechanic as he gleefully punched his calculator.

I also came to realize that I lived more of a truck lifestyle than an SUV lifestyle. Loading building supplies and firewood on a trailer wasn't as easy and convenient as throwing them in the back of a truck. During duck season, I shared the luxurious leather seats with enthusiastic, wet, muddy Labrador retrievers. Then there was deer season. Recently deceased large animals had to be hauled within the cozy confines of that same carpet- and leather-clad interior.

The late summer hail storm that peppered the hood and fenders with dents was the last straw. Winter was coming. I needed to make a decision. Either fix the Ultimate Winter Vehicle or park it at the end of the driveway with a "For Sale" sign in the window.

Now I may be a frugal, stubborn Minnesotan, but it was time to admit defeat. I took the insurance check to a new truck dealer where a polite young salesman listened to my needs. He showed me pictures of his father's cabin two lakes over from mine and we talked about fishing for a while. It was clear that he understood life "Up North" and my dilemma. I allowed him to lead me outside to a new, pretty green, extended cab, four-wheel drive, compact pickup. It was on sale. He was happy to hand over the keys. And a fat monthly payment book.

My backyard storage area still held the pickup topper from the last truck. The color didn't match but it fit just fine. The advertisements in the back of my hunting and fishing magazines provided a bug deflector, camouflage seat covers, and a bed liner via the magic of the Internet. Within a couple of weeks, I had my new "Ultimate Winter Vehicle."

No, it doesn't have an off-road racing suspension, chrome grill guard, or a custom exhaust system. And I will miss the leather interior, the six-disc CD player, the five-passenger seating, that space age dashboard, and my old friend Mick. It does have what experience now tells me is the most important option that any Ultimate Winter Vehicle can have. A bumper-to-bumper, five-year, 50,000 mile warranty.

The Hunters

Youngest son Steve, Ripley the Retriever, and I trudge down the hill in the dark without saying much. It's the third morning of our annual October father/son/dog duck hunt and the early morning wake-ups are starting to wear on us. I know that at least two of us are thinking about the warm sleeping bags we left behind in the cabin. Crooked Lake is waiting for us, shimmering in the starlight of a cloudless night. The old boat is waiting too, tied to the dock with thirty or so artificial ducks loosely piled between the seats. We load the ammo box and cased guns, boost the aging Labrador onto the middle seat, and find our own places amongst the clutter.

Check List—Bow light: ON. Life jackets: ON. Kill switch: ATTACHED. Fuel bulb: PUMPED AND HARD. Choke: OUT. Check list: COMPLETED. I give the little motor's starter rope a hard pull and sink my elbow into Ripley's ribs on the back swing. She grunts but refuses to give up her perch on the middle seat. This is our tenth season together. She trusts that I will adjust and not let it happen again.

The motor fires on the sixth pull. I let it warm up for a few seconds, then back out from the dock and rev the motor to send us skimming off towards the south shore with the distant radio tower blinking red as a guide. The waves, the dim light, and the reflection of the stars combine to form a mesmerizing optical illusion. The boat appears motionless with a river of floating stars rushing past.

Firewood Happens

Duck Island looms ahead out of the dark. I back the motor down and nose the boat into the island. Steve climbs out, trying not to slip on the wet rocks lining the shore. Ripley makes it with one big leap. She won't remember her arthritis until after the day's activities. It's Steve's job to keep her dry while I place the decoys by the light of my headlamp. Sixteen bluebill decoys are arranged in a loose group in the open water on the east side of the island. The rest, mostly fake mallards of various manufacture and vintage, go in the weedy bay on the south side.

With this morning ritual complete, the boat is eased into the shelter of a balsam fir tree. I drape decoy bags over the shiny motor and gas tank, then stumble through the darkness to our makeshift blind of pine branches and marsh grass. Now it's time to relax, pour a first cup of coffee, and listen for early rising ducks in the dawn of a new day. It will be warm, windy, and sunny once the sun clears the eastern shore. Our best chance to fool ducks will be in the early light.

The first ducks arrive shortly after sun-up. Two fast little ringnecks blaze past the decoys from the south, air ripping off their wings. Steve shoulders his 12-gauge pump and gets off one quick shot. The ducks never miss a wing beat and are gone as fast as they came. "Was I behind them?" he asks.

"Who knows," I say. "You just have to let your instincts take over and shoot when things happen that fast."

The next ducks appear on my left, another pair, low to the water and not slowing for the decoys. I start the double barrel to my shoulder as my brain starts the duck ID program. Identifying ducks on the wing is a skill that takes practice—observing different types of ducks as often as possible, looking for little nuances in their shape, flight patterns, and colors. These are small, skinny ducks without much color. The duck ID cards in my brain flip past ringneck and wood duck, and stop at hooded merganser with mental warning bells ringing and lights flashing. They are legal, common, and fast, but not high on the list of edible ducks due to their fishy diet. I lower the gun and warn Steve—"Mergs!" They lift over the trees and drop down into the next lake.

The mergansers prove to be the last ducks of sunrise. The weather is much too nice and the few ducks flying aren't interested in our decoys. That doesn't mean we are bored. Wildlife goes on, on the shores of Crooked Lake.

An immature bald eagle floats over the south shore hoping for dead, injured, or dumb fish. We wonder if it hatched in the nest north of our cabin, riding out last summer's epic Fourth of July storm, perched in a nest sixty feet up in an old white pine, while wind and lightning flattened the forest all around it.

Three otters swim out of the swamp and cruise the small bay, diving, surfacing, sometimes crunching down crayfish for a loud breakfast snack. The shore is littered with piles of otter waste filled with crayfish claws and shells. Ripley loves the stuff. We joke about making a fortune marketing crayfish-flavored dog treats. One of the otters spots us trying to restrain Ripley from diving in after them. All three rise out the water with their front legs bent like miniature mermaids. One loud "CHUFF" and they dive into their watery world and don't reappear.

The sun warms the shallow water of the bay and triggers a feeding frenzy of northern pike and bass swimming among the lily pads. Minnows and small sunfish turn into flying fish, leaping from the water to escape the predators below. Some swim free. Others meet their end in violent splashes, breakfast for some monster of the deep. Maybe I'll be back later with a fishing rod and a floating lure to join in the action.

The sun also wakes up the red squirrel who claims to own this island. He ventures out on a jack pine limb, chastising us with loud squirrel curses. The ruckus lasts for a few minutes; then the busy little creature is bored with us and goes about his business of checking out pine cones. Ripley is bored too. She leaves the blind and sits below the jack pine staring upward at the pest. Steve and I agree she looks like a pampered suburban pooch in her warm camouflage vest. At her age, she deserves special treatment. The squirrel chatters, drops a few pine cones, and pretends to ignore her.

No more ducks show by mid-morning. I have nails to pound back at the cabin and Steve wants to take Ripley into the forest to look for grouse and woodcock. So I leave them in the blind, case my gun, and pole the boat out to collect the decoys. Any experienced duck hunter can guess what happens next.

I pick up the first mallard decoy and start to wind the anchor string, just in time to hear a loud high-pitched whistling. A flock of about thirty ducks makes a quick pass over the decoys and heads out over the main lake. Stubby black and white ducks whose wings are screaming out a constant "whee, whee, whee, whee." Goldeneyes, a.k.a. "whistlers."

Safely out of the line of fire, I quack at them

several times and sit back to watch. This is a decisive bunch of ducks, no endless circling, looking, or calling. They make a quick turn over the lake and come back across the wind, shining black and white in the sun, tipping from side to side to lose altitude while whistling wings announce their arrival. The leaders are starting to touch down when Steve interrupts. The echoing boom from his shotgun sends water flying from wings and shot.

The ducks scramble for altitude in a loose unorganized group. Two more shots boom out in quick succession. The flock swings to the southeast gaining altitude, every one of them still filling the air with the music of their wings. Ripley splashes into the water, swimming through the decoys in search of a floating duck. Steve stands on the shore looking for the same duck. It's not there.

I laugh while Steve makes disparaging remarks about major gun and ammunition manufacturers. Ripley, always quiet and polite, swims back to shore, shakes water from her coat, and keeps her thoughts to herself.

Some would say we had a fruitless morning, maybe even wasted our time. We spent four hours sitting on an island with nothing tangible to show. Trying to explain hunting to a non-hunter is as difficult and unproductive as trying to explain religion to a non-believer. Even a non-hunter who is open-minded will have difficulty understanding or feeling the same emotions we do. It's hard to explain how hunting, at least for me and the hunters I associate with, is not just a casual activity, not a simple passion to kill.

It's a complex mix of senses, emotions, and intangibles. It's not just a flock of ducks knifing through the air in perfect formation, with the air ripping off their wings. It's not just Ripley's collar tags tinkling like bells as she shakes cold lake water on me after a retrieve. It's more than the satisfaction of a well-made shot or the soft warm body of a duck delivered to my hand.

It's these things and more, little secrets that few people other than hunters know or appreciate. Like a bufflehead's feathers shining iridescent green and purple in sunlight. Or reflections in the coal black and shiny bill of a drake gadwall. It's the bite of that first sip of hot, bitter coffee in the dark, cold duck blind. It's Ripley's warm furry body trembling under my hand as we watch a sunlit flock of mallards making one more pass just outside the farthest decoy. Sometimes the best things in life can't be explained. You just know them when you find them.

Their pull is strong. Steve, Ripley, and I will be back tomorrow morning whatever the weather. Weary, bleary-eyed, and waiting for the sound of wings at dawn.

A Friend like Kim

We male cabin owners seem to share several primal urges. Among the most powerful of these is our craving for more and better power tools and the related desire to use them. No cabin project is too big or too complicated for our skills and tools. There's at least one major problem with this. Many of us have something else in common: there's an honest and practical spouse or significant other hanging around.

Nothing can put a damper on a power tool or cabin project dream quicker than one of these naysayers mentioning the chainsawed tree that fell "the left way" instead of "the right way." Or the new storage shed with the crooked roof. Or something really painful like the cut-off cord on the brand new circular saw. When faced with these half-truths, our manly stubbornness and pride often gets in the way of our power tool collections, our construction projects, and our relationships. Here's where I am lucky. I have a friend named Kim.

I met Kim many moons ago at a small northern Minnesota college. We both admit that it was not the educational curriculum that lured us to this institution. It was the college recruiter's pictures of the lake and the pine trees, and the mention of the outdoor sporting opportunities. Kim left school to pursue a practical career in home and cabin construction. I stayed on and headed down a different scientific path. Somehow our relationship withstood the test of time and survived despite the stresses of girlfriends, spouses, families, and even living and working together for a while. To be blunt, I trust Kim. He has his own set of keys to our cabin.

Marcie, my partner in marriage and cabin ownership, also knows and trusts Kim. She has seen his everyday handiwork in the houses he built for his family and in projects like the log siding on "Her" cabin. Kim is a craftsman to be trusted above all unknown contractors, and one known husband, in spite of that time he accidentally on purpose pushed her off the dock fully clothed. Some male cabin owners would be insulted or even feel inadequate given this situation. After all, that famous Canadian phil- osopher, Red Green, keeps telling us—"If the women don't find you handsome, they should at least find you handy." Not me. I have adapted and found ways to benefit from this state of affairs.

Like the time I was trying to decide how to attach steps to the new cabin deck. Only wimps need plans for simple projects like this. I knew I could figure it out, given enough time, a little wasted lumber, maybe several beers, and a few bad words. I was on my own this time. Kim, his thirty years of experience, and his truckload of power tools, weren't available.

Marcie wandered past and inquired, "Why is that taking so long? And why are you doing it 'that' way?"

I resisted the temptation to snap back with a hasty nasty retort. "Because this is how Kim told me to do it," I simply replied. This satisfied her and prevented her from offering her own ideas, which could have been ego-shattering had they been better than mine. She walked away, confident that the steps would be sound and functional in spite of the swearing and lack of progress. A disagreement was averted even though it may have reinforced her image of me as a klutz with a hammer.

There are rewards in addition to maintaining marital harmony. Here's where we get to talk about power tools. My tool rack includes a shiny red and black reciprocating saw. I won't say I worship it, even though it does have a place of honor, right next to the air-nailer, the router, and several other implements of construction. The saw is there because of Kim, even though I paid for it.

I was struggling to handsaw a difficult cut on the framing behind the chimney. This task would have been easier had I not already installed the chimney, thus blocking access, and had I not fired up the stove, thus making the confined space much warmer than it needed to be. Who can think that far ahead? Marcie was sitting nearby in her rocker, wrapped in a blanket, sipping tea, reading, and watching the squirrel fights in the feeders outside. She sensed my frustration in the names I was calling my dull handsaw. "How would Kim do that?" she asked.

"Easy," said I, frustration showing a bit more. "He would pull out his handy dandy, electric, industrial-strength reciprocating saw and be done in about five seconds. But I don't own a #$%^& reciprocating saw!!!!!"

About that time a brilliant idea dawned. I crawled out from behind the chimney, wiped the sweat from my eyes, faced her, and seized upon the situation. "C'mon, we're goin' to town."

She didn't question why. The next step was simple and logical. A short time later she looked on with approval as I picked out the local hardware store's finest name-brand reciprocating saw, complete with protective metal carrying case, extra blades, and an easy twist-lock blade-change system. I swaggered a bit on the walk to the cash register. Price was not an object, not even a consideration. It was what Kim would do.

So, my fellow male cabin owners, I suggest you find a friend like Kim. Someone trustworthy, knowledgeable, and handy, but perhaps only average handsome. Allow him to charm your significant other by fixing that screen door that doesn't close and the pesky leak around the chimney. Show her that a real man, you, her partner, can indeed be capable of asking for guidance and directions. Use his name wisely when he is not available and get his cell phone number for emergencies. The time may come when you need to inform him that he has provided you with sage power tool advice. He needs to know about that new left-hand offset, variable-speed, cordless screwdriver if your wife asks him.

Movin' on Up

While you won't hear much talk about it, a social class system exists up here in the North Country, one that rivals those of medieval times. Like it or not, people fall into four distinct categories that are difficult to escape from.

First there's the ordinary "Tourist"—the lowest on the class totem pole. Tourists show up for a weekend or a week, and then disappear—sometimes forever. One step up are the "Summer People," those who own lake homes or cabins and have the means to spend the summer "Up North" before fleeing south to warmer climates after Labor Day. I fit into the third class—the "Wannabes." We spend many weekends, and a few weeks when possible, at our cabins, four seasons of the year, always hoping to move up to the highest social class—the "Locals."

The locals are a hardy bunch, making a living at everything from farming to banking. Locals come in many shapes, sizes, and nationalities, and are all universally good at one thing. They can spot one of us lower class people a mile away. Some even figure out how to make a buck off us—something that has so far escaped me.

The tourists have the hardest time fitting in. Most are easy to spot with their pale skin and clashing shorts and t-shirts, wandering around town lost, clutching shopping lists. Usually the lists include sunscreen, bug repellent, beer, shiny fishing tackle, and replacements for forgotten swimsuits. A boat or camper hitched to a fancy SUV plastered with "Wall Drug" bumper stickers is another dead giveaway.

The summer people also have a hard time blending in since they hang around all summer and repeatedly use the services offered by locals. The stereotypical summer person is older than most tourists, much better dressed, and prefers to drive an upscale four-door sedan. An older, well-known, male summer person may be referred to as "That Rich Guy From The Cities" by locals. This is not necessarily a derogatory term, although the word "Guy" can be substituted with a less complimentary term if the person is thought to be arrogant and/or tight with his money.

A subset of the summer people deserves mention—the "Summer Girl." Lest you doubt this is a defined term, ask any male local who is or once was a teenager. He will gladly point out nearby examples. These might vary due to personal preference but will likely be well-tanned, well-dressed, attractive young females. Summer girls are a universal fantasy of young male locals. They appear for the warm sunny summer, flash their smiles and good looks around town, and then mysteriously disappear. There may also be "Summer Boys" that keep the young female locals guessing.

That brings us to my "Wannabe" situation. I was a local once, for a while, many years ago. I worked for Jack the Cement Man, played pool at the Legion on Thursday nights against the old guy in the Hawaiian shirt, and helped out at the gas station when Bill needed a break. I could spot tourists, summer people, and especially summer girls, with the best of the locals. Sadly, I had to move south many years ago. For far too long, I was just another tourist. I was able to break free from that sorry state when I built my cabin.

It's unlikely that I will ever be mistaken for a summer person, especially a rich guy from the cities, due to my budget, humble cabin, and lack of style. I do sometimes kid myself that I will fit back in with locals. This fantasy is always burst, just like those old weak attempts at flirting with summer girls.

I pulled into the boat repair shop on a Sunday afternoon with a sick boat. It never occurred to me that my brother-in-law and I won't blend in. Our work clothes were stinky and trashed from a weekend of cabin projects and fishing. The boat wasn't a flashy decked-out ski boat or a glittering bass boat. It was classic 14-foot red Lund, a favorite with the locals. Even so, we never stood a chance. The mechanic listened to the problem description, offered a diagnosis, and quoted a very reasonable price.

"Great," I said. "When will you get to it?"

He replied without hesitation, "I'll make sure it's ready when you come back up for Memorial Day." Clearly I wasn't a summer person or a rich guy from the cities. And I wasn't a local who would need the boat ASAP. Maybe I should be happy that he didn't mistake me for a lowly tourist.

I'm not sure how many years it will take to become a local if we retire to the cabin. Blending in would probably mean spending time hanging out at the coffee shop, helping with church functions, joining the VFW, and maybe working part-time, helping some business separate money from the tourists and summer people. Sometimes I do have hope.

The other day I was wandering the aisles of the hardware store when a tourist stopped me. He was "not from around here." He had the whole sunburn, shorts, sandals, t-shirt, glazed eye thing going. "Say," he asked. "Where can I get a propane tank filled around here?"

I didn't have to think. "Head west about five blocks to the stoplight. The gas station on the northwest corner has a bulk tank and fills 'em cheap."

"Thanks!" He walked away happy, pleased with himself, satisfied that he had tapped into local knowledge.

It wasn't much of a challenge, helping out a hapless tourist. However, I was gloating a bit as I plopped my mousetraps and birdseed down on the checkout counter and struck up a conversation with the local gal behind it. "Seems pretty busy in here today."

"Yeah," she replied. "There's lots of you 'Cabin People' up here this weekend."

Firewood Happens

I believe every Northwoods home or cabin should have a real wood stove—not just one of those gas fireplaces with the fake logs. A good EPA-approved wood burner with a top-of-the-line chimney won't be cheap and your insurance agent might cringe and whine when you mention it. Don't worry. There are other agents who understand the situation. Here in the woods, firewood happens.

Firewood happens when Mother Nature's thunderstorms and blizzards rearrange the forest, weeding out the weak and unfortunate, sending firewood falling from the sky like manna from heaven. We can waste time arguing about whether or not the trees make a sound when they fall. However, we do know that they will land on the cabin or the outhouse or the boat. This will make that insurance agent whine even more. Forget him for the moment and deal with the firewood.

Firewood can happen in less painful ways. The easiest, and arguably the most expensive, is to simply scan the local newspaper for suppliers. A phone call or two will result in the delivery of an ample supply already cut, split, dried, and ready for the stove. While this method helps the economy and local entrepreneurs, writing a check for firewood does not provide enough adventure for me. I like to hunt mine down.

Hunting wild firewood is a legitimate option. State and national forests allow firewood collection subject to regulations and permit conditions. Leftovers from logging activities are prime candidates. All you need is a permit, a sturdy truck, several chainsaws, and a well-stocked first aid kit. A talk with the aforementioned insurance agent about truck insurance, health insurance, and life insurance might also be a good idea.

Foraging for firewood is an adventure similar to prospecting for precious metals. You might strike it rich with a mother lode of naturally dried oak, right next to the road. Or you could strike out with a light load of semi-rotten aspen, a broken chainsaw, and an expensive towing bill from getting too adventurous. I've soured on this method given adventures like these and the fact that the prime firewood gathering season happens to coincide with fishing season, duck season, grouse season, and deer season.

When my supply of homegrown firewood gets low, I now scrounge local sawmills to see what type of slab wood is available. Slab wood is the exterior wood and bark left over from slicing small boards out of full logs. Every slab is different. Length and thickness depend on the quality of the parent log. A straight log will turn out boring slabs of consistent length and thickness. A crooked log will provide thin pieces for kindling and thicker, slower-burning chunks for long winter nights. All you have to do is get it back to the cabin, cut it into stove-sized pieces, stack, and dry. Depending on the source, it can be cheap, even if you pay for delivery. Higher tech sawmills now cut it to length and dump off truckload quantities, along with a bigger bill.

One word of caution. Stacking too many thin pieces of slab wood in a stove makes for a very hot fire due to the increased surface area of the slab. This can cause a chimney fire, or even a stove meltdown if you bought a wood burner on clearance at a discount store. The end result may be an embarrassing talk with that unhappy insurance agent.

A second word of caution. Every other piece of slab wood you pull from the pile will be a natural work of art, begging to be a craft project instead of a lowly piece of firewood. Take my advice here: spend a moment admiring the beauty of nature's handiwork—the distressed contrasting wood grain, the strategically placed knotholes, and the interesting worm and bug channels. Then place it on your sawbuck and promptly make firewood happen. Winter is coming and you are a cabin owner. You need firewood and heat much more than a shed full of craft projects that will never get crafted.

This method of making firewood happen sounds simple enough and results in plenty of quality time with your chainsaw without having to experience the hazards of cutting down trees or foraging in the dark and dangerous forest. It doesn't have to be. Seeking out firewood bargains from small, private sawmills requires an adventurous soul willing to drive miles down pot-holed and wash-boarded back roads, hot on the trail of rumored stacks of seasoned slab oak.

One such snowy December adventure led me to a small sawmill on a family farm. A Shepherd-Lab-crossbreed-mutt farm dog rose from the porch to greet me as I exited my truck. Many years of knocking on farm house doors to deal with sensitive environmental issues have left me leery of this specific type of dog. This one was an exception. It greeted me with a wagging tail and a full mouth, offering to share the grisly leftovers of its master's recent deer hunt. I politely declined and continued on to the back door with my new friend.

A shadowy figure waved from a side window and motioned me to enter. The door opened to an entry way/mud room cluttered with the accumulated debris of early winter rural life. Warm boots with liners pulled out and drying, well-used shotguns and deer rifles half-exposed in unzipped cases, worn work coats, overalls, gloves, hats, and jackets hanging from hooks and draped across old chairs. A hollered "Come on in— I'm on the phone!" greeted me from farther back in the house.

The mystery figure was in the kitchen, in the

midst of cooking a hearty breakfast with one hand, while holding a cordless phone and doing business with the other. This was no high-class joint. The cook's uniform was an old hooded sweatshirt of blue plaid flannel, farm store jeans, and a dark baseball hat, no doubt a freebie from a local business. It didn't matter. Breakfast smelled just fine. A flannel-clad arm motioned me to the kitchen table and poured me a cup of coffee as the phone call ended. Then we got down to introductions and business.

"Hey," he said, sticking out the non-spatula hand. "I'm Kenny. How'd you like your eggs?"

It took most of two hours to close the deal on a couple bundles of birch slabs for the stove and fire pit. As it turns out, Kenny (name changed to protect the not-so-innocent) and I had a lot in common. Most of the time was spent swapping stories of growing up on rural Minnesota farms with large flocks of siblings, lots of work, plenty of food, and little else. Thrown in for good measure were a few good deer hunting tales and a couple of new (at least to me), very creative, very earthy sayings that can't be repeated in a family setting.

I left the farm smiling, only slightly poorer in money, much richer in firewood, and certainly not hungry. Yes, firewood does happen. And this time it came with bacon and eggs.

Dock Tales

My neighbors probably consider me cheap and lazy when it comes to docks. Two cabins to the east, Marv has two—a conventional roll-in with covered boat-lift and a unique drawbridge affair that cranks up out of the water at the end of the summer. Just next door, Tom has an expensive, plastic-decked, adjustable roll-in complete with benches, beverage holders, and a rainbow-colored windsock flapping in the breeze. My homemade wooden dock pales by comparison. I haven't even bothered to take it out for the winter in years.

I have my reasons for this low-cost, low-effort dock philosophy. Some are practical considerations. Like not wanting to get my feet wet on early morning duck hunts right before freeze up. The dogs, sons, other assorted freeloaders, and I load the boat from the comfort of the dock and head out with dry feet. Need a place to change into your cross-country skis once the lake turns solid? Come on over to my iced-in dock and have a seat. Want to be the first to cast a hook and bobber to open water in the spring? No problem. My dock is already in.

I also find that "things" tend to happen on docks. Things stories are made of. The longer the dock is in, the more things happen, and the more I have to write. Like the late April morning when Marcie, Ripley the Retriever, and I tried to squeeze onto the end platform to catch the makings of a spring fish fry.

Marcie stepped to the left to avoid the dripping wet Labrador. One step too far to the left. She stood for a moment with left foot off the dock, in empty air, flailing her arms, trying to maintain balance.

Blocked by the same wet mutt, I could do little to help without endangering my own warm, dry self. I did reach over and rescue the fishing rod from her hand before she succumbed to the laws of gravity, and splashed down into four feet of thirty-three degree water. The dog and I were worried for a moment. Then she surfaced laughing, and we added one more story to the cabin journal.

The dock serves as my all-season psychiatrist's couch, with the lake and nature as my therapists. I went there often during the first years we owned the undeveloped lot. There I wrestled with inner demons named Mortgage Payment, Property Tax, and Sweat Equity. It was a place to reflect on the decision to spend limited resources on five acres of Minnesota northwoods jungle that provided more bug bites and poison ivy blisters than idyllic summer moments.

I have long since sent those demons packing. Still I try to visit the dock at the end of each visit, to see the lake one more time, to hear the ospreys chirping high above in the updrafts, or to hear one last loon yodel. This last little bit of dock time helps carry me through the long drive home and the wait for the next trip. And "things" continue to happen on the dock.

On an early November day I packed my gear into the truck and headed down the hill, fishing rod in hand, for one last look at an unfrozen lake, one more appointment with the therapists. I cast a few times from the end of the dock, not really fishing, just passing time, enjoying the quiet lake and pondering the passing of the seasons.

My reflections on life were interrupted when a silver flash of a fish rocketed out of the bull rushes and slammed into the lure within feet of the dock. Surprised, I held on to the rod with both hands as line ripped off the reel and out into the lake. It wasn't a fair fight—I never had a chance. This sneaky aquatic juggernaut tangled in some solid object and left me firmly snagged with no sign of life at the end of the line.

It was tempting to take the easy way out, to snap the line and sacrifice a six-dollar lure to the lake gods. My only other option, short of an icy swim, was Marcie's blue and white paddleboat resting upside down on the dock. I flipped it into the water with my free hand, climbed into the wet seat, and pedaled out to attempt a retrieve.

When the line was pointing straight down, I leaned over the side, hoping for a glimpse of my red and white lure. And there it was, wrapped around a sunken tree branch, still attached to the jaws of a big unhappy northern pike.

We all know that both fishermen and water magnify size. In this case you have my solemn oath that the nasty-looking critter at the end of the line was at least three feet long and had to weigh at least ten pounds. He/she would easily have been the biggest dock fish of the year. I cranked hard on the reel, spraying water as I back-pedaled to tighten the line. The fish shook its head, snapped the line, and was gone into the clear depths of Crooked Lake.

I was left with a broken line, cursing like a sailor on a much bigger boat. That big-one-that-got-away funk didn't last long. I was laughing on the paddle back to the cheap little dock. Marv and Tom may have spent more money on their docks, but money can't buy memories like these.

The Ol' Red
and White

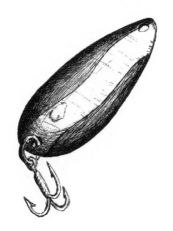

Oldest son Andy has grown tired of fishing on Crooked Lake. "Too dang many slimy northern pike. Why don't we ever fish for walleyes on another lake?"

At the risk of sounding like an old codger, I'm tempted to remind him how fortunate he is. He's lived his entire life in a household with at least one boat, plenty of modern fishing gear, week-long vacations, and a lake lot or cabin since he was thirteen.

I never had it that good. Growing up a poor Minnesota farm boy meant being deprived of many things. Things like TV, indoor plumbing, store-bought toys, and real fishing tackle. When I headed down to the "crik" to worry the carp and bullheads, all my rusty green tackle box held were a couple of hooks and a handful of rusty washers and nuts for fishing weights. If there happened to be an actual fishing lure in that box, it was a red and white spoon with rusted treble hooks, a hand-me-down from Dad.

This lure was the star of one of my earliest "the big one that got away" fishing memories. I walked down the dusty gravel road to the bridge over Spring Creek one summer morning, tied on my one and only red and white spoon, and hauled back on my prized blue fiberglass rod. The lure sailed up the creek with the old bait-casting reel screaming in protest and splashed down at the head of the pool. It was instantly snatched by a powerful force. I struck back and watched, open-mouthed, as a huge northern pike leaped clear of the water with the lure clenched in its jaws. It hung in the air for an eternity, broke my rotten black line with a shake of its head, and splashed back into the muddy creek. "My" fish and that red and white spoon were gone and not seen again.

The occasional and much-awaited weekend trips "Up North" were filled with fishing with Dad and his big friend Denny. Northern pike were plentiful and always ready to strike the red and whites as we trolled in a rented resort boat. Sometimes the boat was powered with a loud outboard motor belching blue smoke. Sometimes Denny manned the oars, moving us along weedy green shores with the power of his farmer-strong shoulders.

The only problem I remember was the lack of a landing net, an expensive accessory no one seemed to own. Time and time again, I would fight a toothy green and white northern to the boat, only to watch it thrash back into the water as Dad or Denny grabbed the line and tried to flop it in. I guess it was an early method of catch and release. Any fish that found its way into the boat was headed straight to the stringer, then the resort fish-cleaning shack, and finally the frying pan.

Now I am blessed with perhaps too many boats and a brother-in-law in the fish tackle business who is generous with samples. There are lures in my stockpile that will never see the water. Nevertheless, I recently succumbed to a fit of nostalgia when I spotted a red and white spoon at the local bait store. Six bucks seemed like a lot of money for a shaped and painted hunk of metal. Still, it was a "name brand" and I guess even nostalgia has a price.

Back at the cabin, I picked through my arsenal of fishing rods and selected a cheap bait-casting outfit, the closest thing to that blue fiberglass rod from earlier days. I lugged coffee cup, tackle box, and rod down to the dock and climbed into the old 14-foot Starcraft with the dog. The six-horse fired on the first pull and I set out trolling down memory lane with a few ghosts of fishing trips past on board. What would I have taken up for a hobby if Dad and his friends hadn't taken me along fishing when they had a moment to relax?

I sailed the lure back about fifty feet, picked out the backlash, and headed east along the shore, enjoying the pleasantly cool summer evening. I didn't have to go far. A fish slammed into the lure right at the best spot on the lake, straight out in front of Marv and Marie's dock.

The fight was not as spectacular as that of my childhood fish in the creek at the farm. This northern stayed deep, doggedly shaking his head as I brought him close. He did the typical splash-and-run several times at boat side, just to worry the dog and me. Once again, a net wasn't handy; they always seem to be somewhere else. Other than that, my biggest problem was the nosy Labrador retriever trying to push me out of the way to help. I avoided the teeth, grabbed the fish behind the gills and lifted him into the boat.

Large he was not. At eighteen or nineteen or twenty inches or so, he was long and thick enough to not qualify as a "hammer handle." I admired his spots and his toothy grin, allowed the dog to lick him once, and then lowered him back into the water. He managed to splash me good as he swirled and was gone. I didn't really mind. My six-dollar investment had paid off. What a small price to pay to feel like a kid again.

The Curse of
Boat Addiction

The light of the traditional fishing opener campfire reflected off the cabin's log siding, illuminating the faces of the men of the family in a warm glow. It was late and the Patriarch was waxing eloquent to a captive assortment of sons, sons-in-law, and grandsons after returning from wintering in the sunny, waterless desert of the Southwest. "Arizonians don't have the faintest idea about how we feel about boats here in Minnesota," he stated. "My friends down there don't believe me when I tell them how many boats we have in this family. They can't imagine why a man needs more than one."

Those of us at the fire nodded our heads in silent agreement. For once the old man knew what he was talking about. I nursed my beer in the flickering light of the campfire and reflected back to the day nearly thirty years ago when I first realized he suffered from an incurable affliction called "Boat Addiction."

Marcie and I were cruising home down Highway 169 when we overtook an old Chevy Impala, limping along with a boat and trailer in tow. Both trailer wheels were slanted outwards on a bent axle, wobbling furiously, and threatening to spin off the hubs. A faded blue and white fiberglass runabout sat crooked on the trailer with an outboard of questionable age hanging off the transom.

Marcie turned to me, laughing. "THAT looks like something your dad would buy!" These words rang true as we pulled alongside, looked at the driver, and waved hello to Dad.

You might not find a description of boat addiction in any medical dictionary. Yet the signs and symptoms are well known anywhere in lake country. The early stages seem harmless enough. The afflicted person slows down and pulls over to read "For Sale" signs on used boats parked along streets and roads. The first dangerous thoughts begin to creep into his or her mind. "That's not a bad deal!" they might say, a sure sign that trouble is brewing.

These thoughts and words evolve and become increasingly illogical as the disease progresses. A person reaches the mature stages of the addiction when he or she states, "I could fix that up, sell it, and make a bundle." Words lead to action and a wreck of a boat comes home to clog the garage, driveway, or backyard for years. The final stages of this condition take many forms. They may involve old boats, many boats, big boats, expensive boats, or various combinations of all of the above. There is good news. Boat addiction is rarely fatal. Then again, there is bad news. Empty bank accounts and marital discord are common symptoms.

My father did learn to partially control his problem. Although he did own a series of embarrassing junkers—hulking fiberglass cruisers sporting strange pastel colors—he never owned more than two at a time. My siblings and I thought he was cured when he rid himself of them and purchased a new boat with a reliable engine, a solid floor, and a trailer without a bent axle. Then came last summer. That's when he took possession of an old pea-green fiberglass bass boat that a neighbor offered him for free.

Trust me on this one—buying a new boat rarely proves to be a high return investment. Assuming ownership of a "free" boat is always a losing proposition. One of the females of the family (who shall remain nameless) took one look and offered this assessment—"That's not a boat—that's a flower planter!"

While many of us agreed with this appraisal, we felt compelled to help when he enlisted all available sons and grandsons to move the ugly beast. I surveyed the situation and saw nothing wrong with its current resting place next to a large brush pile. I had to question the obvious. "Dad, why are we moving it? Nobody's going to steal it."

"They're going to burn the brush pile," he replied. "I don't want it to get scorched."

As he turned away, one of my sons (who shall also remain nameless), looked to me and made a suggestion. "Let's throw it on top of the pile." Thankfully his grandfather had the hearing aids turned down and remained oblivious to the comment. I was proud of my son. He recognized the symptoms of boat addiction at an early age. He may escape the family curse.

Yes, boat addiction has become a family curse. While my youngest brother seems to have escaped it by moving to the mountains of Colorado, those of us who stayed behind have not been so lucky. My middle brother has a large, needy, thirty-year-old sailboat docked on Lake Superior. The five-hour drive to and from the marina keeps him occupied half the year. The other half he spends crafting beautiful wood kayaks and canoes in his home garage—and repairing parts of the sailboat.

My personal addiction is a straightforward numbers kind of thing. It started in 1977 when Marcie and I spent most of our first tax return on a new aluminum canoe. A small used fishing boat, complete with a used JCPenney outboard motor, came along several years later. The lesson learned from this folly was to buy clothing from JCPenney—not boat motors.

I learned little else. Soon a new 17-foot fish-and-ski boat was added to the fleet after an ill-advised trip to a boat show. Then building our lake cabin fueled the fires of this terrible addiction. Another old fishing boat and a new paddleboat were needed for summer fun. Next? Early last spring, brother-in-law Darv mentioned that a coworker was desperate to sell a slightly used Lund with an almost new motor. What sane Minnesotan would pass up a deal on a Lund?

My addiction has not gone unnoticed. Earlier that day a good friend pulled up to the cabin with a faded yellow canoe loaded in his pickup. "It's been laying around the farm for years," Neil told me. "I figured you might have a use for it."

Yes, I helped him unload it—even stood back to admire the new acquisition and think happy thoughts of all the summer fun to be had. I guess that makes it number seven. But then who's counting?

Night of the Creeper

Trust me—you don't want to sit near me and watch a good old-fashioned horror movie. I'm a sucker for suspense. It doesn't matter how many times I've seen the movie or one like it, I'll still jump in my seat when the monster, or crazed madman, or werewolf, or vampire shows. Given these issues, there's at least one other activity you should avoid doing with me— muskie fishing at night.

On a clear August night, my brother-in-law Dale conned a colleague in the fishing tackle business into taking us muskie fishing. I've fished for muskies before—even caught one once. Yet targeting them in the dark of a summer night had a certain strange appeal. I went along with the idea, much like the tag-along kid in all those old movies who follows his friends into a creepy abandoned house while the audience yells—"Don't do it!!!"

Disclaimer: Kids and adults—don't try this on your own without professional help. The price of the tackle alone is more that the price of a good guide. And believe me, you will need him. Not just to find fish and provide tackle, but to find your way back to the boat landing at midnight. This was especially true for us as the boat left the landing on Big Mantrap Lake. No secret here—Mantrap is well known as a world-class muskie lake. There is also a reason for the name. A man could be trapped for days in this lake's maze of islands, channels, and dead-end bays. A woman, on the other hand, would probably ask any of the cabin owners or other anglers for directions and be just fine.

We launched with several hours of daylight left so Dale and I could be acclimated to the tackle and techniques. Dane, our guide for the evening, gave us a quick tour of the hotspots and basic instructions on the tackle. The rods and lures seemed more suited to wrestling a great white shark than anything that lived in a Minnesota lake. The size and heft of the tackle soon had me wishing I'd been lifting weights for several years and had carpal tunnel and rotator cuff surgery to boot. Dane soon showed us he knew this sport. We had just started casting when a small tiger muskie of ten or fifteen pounds stalked his curly tailed plastic lure back to the boat, hanging back like a werewolf in the shadows, biding time before the kill, choosing at the last moment to vanish back into the dark depths and seek other prey.

Mantrap has everything a muskie could want for habitat—deep water, shallow water, weed beds, sunken islands, and underwater points. Dane pointed them out while delivering a running lesson in the finer points of muskie fishing and lures. He started me out with a classic muskie lure—a bucktail spinner. It's an effective lure and easy to use. It's also boring. You heave it out, reel it straight back in, make it do a figure eight in the water at boat side, and then repeat again, and again, and again. Dane must have sensed that I was getting bored as darkness approached. He handed me a rod with a huge wood and metal frog-colored monstrosity dangling from the end.

"Try the Creeper," he said.

I flung the strange thing out about half a mile, picked the backlash out of the reel, started cranking, and immediately knew what the Creeper was all about. The metal blades on each side of the wood body flailed at the water exactly like a flightless duckling frantically flapping across the water to escape harm.

The Creeper beat a loud perfect rhythm back to the boat just like a succulent young teenager crashing through dark woods, screaming, trying to escape a vampire in a B movie. Every muskie within one hundred yards must have known the Creeper was out there. Excuse the expression, but this was cool.

Dane handed my brother-in-law a rod with another top-water lure. This one had a propeller on the rear that sputtered across the top of the water making an equally enticing noise. The suspense grew as the night got darker and the lake grew calm. The only thing missing was a full moon and a howling wolf. Then again, the loons wailing in the distance and the three-quarter moon added plenty to the ambiance. The monsters that lurked in Mantrap waited just long enough to lull us into a false sense of security and then attacked.

Keep in mind three of us were casting big dangerous lures from a small boat, in the dark, with just enough lights to be legal. We were on edge and easy targets. I was standing on the back casting platform, cranking the reel and listening to the Creeper flap back to the boat. Dale's sputtering lure came alongside as he reeled from the middle. It was perhaps three feet from me when a monster muskie exploded out of the water and pounced on the lure with savage intent.

I screamed like a teenaged girl who has just seen her first and last vampire, added in some manly bad words, and had to stop myself from jumping out the other side of the boat. The fish was gone just as quickly, not hooked in the sudden violent attack. My hair stood on end while my heart tried to beat its way out of my chest. This was better than any old monster movie. I was hooked (not literally) and started thinking about converting a boat and buying tackle of my own.

I wish that we had continued on that night and caught many huge, mean fish from Mantrap. But as usually happens when muskie fishing, we didn't catch even one fish. There was more excitement. Dale had a second sudden violent hit farther from the boat. Still another muskie repeatedly jumped and thrashed in the calm summer night, mad at the world and us, ready to fight. Still on edge, I continued to fling the Creeper out, anticipating that bad things could happen at any moment.

The final thrill came as we quit for the night. You know the part in all those scary movies where the hero or victim hears or senses something in the dark and investigates with a dim flashlight or candle? You know something horrible is waiting, yet once again you jump in your seat when the monster suddenly shows.

Dane put down his rod, aimed his flashlight over the side of the boat, and flipped it on. There, hovering near my now quiet Creeper, was the star of many a small fish's nightmares. A muskie he later estimated to be over fifty inches long, a real trophy, hung motionless just below the surface. It stared up at me, evil eyes gleaming in the light, pointed teeth grinning from its jaws, waiting.

I screamed like a girl again.

Damn Dogs

Oldest son Andy, old dog Ripley, five-month-old puppy Kaliber, and I watched the October sun sink into the pines from the island duck blind. The veteran Ripley stared out over her grizzled muzzle at the decoys and tried to ignore the pest of a puppy who did not seem to understand the serious business of waterfowl hunting. Andy and I did our best to amuse the pup while we enjoyed a rare afternoon together. Hunting and fishing time had been hard to find since he started college. Everything was fine until the ducks showed up.

A single ringneck, the most common duck on Crooked Lake, rounded the point of the island and made a screaming dive over the decoys. I managed to react in time and tumbled the duck to the water with the first shot from the double barrel. The puppy escaped Andy, launched herself into the frigid water, and was fast on her way to the duck, whining with excitement as she paddled. Before I could lower the gun, another half dozen ringnecks followed in the same flight path as the single. One more duck splashed into the water with my second shot. Two in a row. A rare feat for me.

Ripley stood belly-deep in the water, tail drooping, watching Kaliber's retrieve. She knew from a summer's worth of dock games that her old bones and worn-out muscles were no match for the skinny, half-grown youngster. I got her attention and pointed towards the second bird, floating closer in the decoys. "It's ok, old girl. There's one for you, too."

She lumbered out into the lake and made the retrieve without further urging, delivering the drab gray and white duck back to shore and, as was her habit, dropping it on the first dry ground. Andy was waiting for her, petting and praising his elderly best friend.

I turned my attention to the puppy, hoping to gain some control over this free spirit as she finished the longer retrieve. She delivered the bird to hand, just like one of the thousands of sticks, tennis balls, and Frisbees she fetched from the dock during the summer, then bounced off to look for more. I would have paid more attention to Ripley had I known it would be her last retrieve. My companion of eleven years had to be carried up the hill to the cabin that evening. She never hunted again.

I don't want to imagine hunting, or life, without a Labrador retriever. While some hunters choose to keep their dog in a backyard kennel, only to be used as a tool to flush and fetch, many more of us pick a puppy from a squirming pack of noisy fun and take it home to become a full-fledged member of the family. There's a problem with this—the damn dog's short life. It's not the dog's fault. Yet I can't refrain from cursing as every one of them inevitably dies in my arms in the veterinarian's exam room.

The family was with me the next spring at the cabin on a cool, misty spring morning. Andy, Steve, Marcie, and I cried as we spread some of Ripley's ashes around the yard where she guarded the bird feeders from marauding squirrels and chipmunks. We cast the rest off the dock among the curious sunfish that frustrated her retrieving instincts for all those summers. Yet it was difficult to dwell on the past, even on that dreary day. There with us the entire time was year-old Kaliber, tennis ball in mouth, begging us to play.

Yes, that energetic black puppy will put us through these same pains. But while I may curse all my dogs for their too-short lives, I always remember to thank God for Labrador puppies.

Why?

Why?

Stray snowflakes flicker out of the darkness, crossing the headlamp beam as I search out my usual seat on Duck Island. The decoys are set and the boat is tucked away on the backside of the island. Now there's time to pour a cup of coffee and relax for fifteen or twenty minutes before shooting time. Time to let my mind wander and once again try to answer why I come here, duck hunting, on this little island in Crooked Lake, at 6:30 a.m. on a cold October morning.

It's not a comfort thing. "Comfort" would be back at my cozy cabin, still in bed, with a few chunks of homegrown, hand-split, seasoned oak glowing away in the wood stove. The cabin could be eighty degrees inside if I wanted. So why am I sitting out here at twenty degrees with the snowflakes drifting down my neck?

Maybe it's the stargazing. They were blazing earlier before the clouds moved in. I really should take time to learn more of the constellations. The Big Dipper is easy. From there on I coin my own names. The Fish Spear is my favorite. It's a trident-shaped cluster of stars, dead center and medium high on the southern horizon. Marcie says they're probably part of Orion's Belt. Whatever. I like Fish Spear better.

It's not the companionship, at least the human kind. I'm by myself this morning with only the dog for company. That's the way I prefer it, today anyway. No pressure to play guide for friends, sons, nephews, or in-laws. Just myself to worry about, with no obligations, and only my own wandering thoughts.

It could be the dog. Kaliber, the current Labrador-Retriever-in-Residence, sure feels good lying across my lap. She doesn't seem to know or care that Labrador retrievers aren't meant to be lapdogs. It's a good thing she weighs in at fifty-five pounds—not the seventy-five or eighty my other Labs have. She's quiet and still for the time being, so I put up with her warm body sprawled across me. Silky soft ears and warm dry fur. The ice around the edge of the lake won't stop this crazy little dog once the ducks show up. Thank God for her Neoprene coat. The guy that invented these should be inducted into the Hunting Dog Hall of Fame if there is one.

It's certainly not the food. That's for sure. I'm already sick of juice boxes and granola bars for breakfast. But I had better learn to tolerate the menu. There's plenty of duck season left and then come three or four long weekends of deer hunting. Bacon from the local meat market, a couple of sunny-side-up eggs, and a slice or two of whole-grain wheat toast would be nice. I'd have to crawl out of bed even earlier to make that happen. Way too much earlier.

It might be the coffee. The dark black liquid in my Thermos is simple stuff from a can, brewed in my combination alarm clock/coffee maker back at the cabin. It may not be three-dollar-a-cup designer latte but it sure tastes good as the eastern sky turns pink and the temperature takes that last little dip before sunrise. I just hope the dog doesn't spill it once the action starts.

I suppose I could come here just to watch the sunrise. The sky is clearing to the east and the random snowflakes seem to have stopped. The sun is turning the eastern sky a rosy purple as it tries to force its way through the clouds and the thin row of birch and pines on Stony Point. The combination of subtle reflections and muted colors on the mirror-calm lake approaches the indescribable—one of those you-had-to-be-there-to-see-it sunrises. Once again I wish for a decent camera that I wasn't afraid to take on these excursions. Delicate things like expensive cameras tend to get wet, dirty, and broke when you hunt ducks in late October with a dog, just south of Canada. The cheapie in my backpack will have to do once the scene brightens.

And I'm sure not here to play with expensive, elaborate equipment. The side-by-side 12-gauge shotgun resting next to me is solid and functional, not a work of art. It's less than ten years old and prematurely aging from this cold, wet waterfowling. I like the look of it, the fit, and the three-and-a-half inch chambers just in case a stray goose wanders by. My decoys aren't perfect either. Six of "these," five of "those," maybe a dozen of "them." Whatever looked good and was on sale. Hopefully they're all still floating at the end of the morning. Shooting at low-flying ducks tends to be hard on high-floating decoys.

Maybe it's the ducks? A flock just sliced through the air above me. Couldn't see them against the sky in the dim predawn. Sounded like a small flock of divers making a five-minutes-before-shooting-time run across the lake. Probably ringnecks or maybe an early flight of bluebills fresh in from Lake of the Woods. They're tough targets when they dive down over the decoys and zoom up at the last minute like miniature jet fighters on a strafing run. The dog heard them too and now we're both keyed up. She retrieved her first duck when only four months old and knows what's up. She stirs from my lap and sits alongside me, trembling with a combination of cold and anticipation.

Or maybe it's the humor. Four mergansers skid into the dimly lit water just outside the decoys. Two of them can't figure out what Kaliber is and swim in to investigate, only feet away, turning spiked head feathers back and forth, staring at the quivering, whining, black "Thing" on shore. She can't take the stress, ignores my whispered commands, and pounces from the bank. They dive under in panic, then erupt out of the water like rockets fired from a submarine. I can't help laughing at the bad doggie etiquette, even though I'm about to have a shivering, cold, wet lapdog.

So I wonder again what brings me here, as Kaliber shakes icy water over me, the gun, and the coffee, her collar tags tinkling a bell-like melody. But I better not wonder long. A black and white reflection just moved across the dark water, accompanied by the distinctive whistling of a goldeneye's wings.

I imagine the duck pirouetting over the lake, cupping its wings, and gliding in out of the dawning sun. It's time to quit wondering why, to slide the safety off on the double barrel, and whisper to the trembling dog beside me. Maybe I'll find an answer in the coming flurry of action. Then again, maybe I will be back tomorrow to give it some more thought.

Holding on to Winter

After four months of ice and snow, you might assume that most people living "Up North" have had enough of winter. Maybe so, but don't include me in this crowd. I'm not quite ready for spring. The book isn't ready to pitch to publishers, the last few pieces of cabin woodwork need to be cut and fitted, and next year's firewood hasn't split itself. More important, there's still fun to be had.

I grab one of the pairs of skis leaning against the cabin's log siding and follow the dog down the hill to the lake. The small wooden dock still stretches out from the frozen shore, locked in the grip of two feet of ice. I offer no apologies for my assumed laziness. The dock is a great place to sit and watch ice fishing tip-ups, to listen to the lake boom and groan as it makes more ice, or to stargaze on a crisp clear winter night. It also makes a semi-dry seat while I lace up ski boots and step into the bindings. Kaliber bounces in anticipation while I finish. She's ready to run.

Pushing away from the dock, the lean black dog and I cross the narrow channel to Big Island, duck under the red pine leaning off the eastern tip, and head straight across the barren white expanse of the lake toward the island-studded south shore. The warmer pre-spring temperatures have changed the snow to a slick, crystal-like consistency. My "back country" skis, wider and shorter than traditional touring skis, slide like skates on fresh ice. I glide straight ahead, poling, kicking, seeking that perfect rhythm of muscles and skis. Kal quarters in front, zigzagging with her nose to the snow, happy to be free from the confines of the cabin.

We had the lake to ourselves when we skied this route three weeks ago. The colder temperatures and crusted snow kept wildlife from roving and marring the clean-slate snow with their tracks. Now subtle signs of the coming spring are showing along the shores. Small puddles of melt water collect on the ice wherever a pine branch bends close, reflecting the new warmth of the sun. Deer, mink, and fisher are drawn to these oases in the winter desert and leave strings of tracks for the dog to nose and follow. Even last fall's wayward leaves and pine cones act as solar collectors, melting matched silhouettes down into the sugar snow.

With the help of the skis and the winter ice, it's possible to explore the bog area between the south shore and the islands. Beaver channels dredged though the tamarack trees and sphagnum moss become narrow, natural ski trails. The bog will be impossible to visit once spring comes—a no man's land of blood-sucking mosquitoes and strange, bug-eating plants. A quaking, fragile surface ready to swallow intruders down into the dark, bottomless depths of tea-stained water.

Out of the bog and following the uneven shoreline east to Stony Point, I pick up speed on the open ice. The dog rummages along the shore, periodically breaking out and racing ahead. She stops to roll in some questionable-looking yellow snow before ducking back into the cattails and brush. Hopefully the wild perfume she found irresistible will fade away by the time we return to the cabin.

The ice pressure ridge across the narrows of Stony Point has become a victim of solar energy. Rocks just below the surface, warmed in the sun, melted the icy upheaval bulging between the points, and collapsed it to open a narrow sliver of water. The otters like the fishing access. Fish scales and crayfish parts are scattered around in testimony to their success. Three-toed raven tracks mix in with the otter sign, the ravens scavenging through the leftovers. The beavers have been busy too, using these small cracks in the frozen armor of the lake to launch forays against the birch and aspen on the point. Their hut down the shore looks like the beaver version of a luxury mansion.

Distant honking alerts us to a final sign of spring. A ragged formation of Canada geese appears over the far shoreline and cruises north across the bay, silhouetted in the crystal blue sky. The flock clears the pines on Stony Point and continues up the lake, doing their best to imitate a Francis Lee Jaques drawing from *The Geese Fly High*.

Dog and man admire the view as they fade into the distance. Then I push off and continue up the shore, Kal once again quartering ahead, enjoying the freedom of the skis, the ice, the snow—holding on to winter while we can.

A Morel Moment

A Morel Moment

One of the benefits of a cabin on the edge of thousands of acres of state forest is being able to walk out the front door or the back door and begin foraging for wild edible plants. Some, like wild asparagus, are easy to identify but hard to find. Wild asparagus looks pretty much like grocery store asparagus and, to my knowledge, has no deadly look-alike. Finding it amongst the poison ivy of road ditches and lake banks is another story.

Others are easy to find and identify, coming with another type of hazard warning. Wander the edge of a clear cut or a forest road in midsummer. Wild raspberries will be there for the picking. Just be ready for the ticks, mosquitoes, deer flies, horse flies, and bears that might be out foraging with you—or on you.

Of all these tasty things, mushrooms hold the most mystique, due to the dire consequences of mistaken identity. Most people would rather hold up a lightning rod in a boat in the middle of a lake during a thunderstorm than eat a wild mushroom. These people would be missing out on the tasty springtime treat of the morel mushroom. These can be identified and enjoyed with minimal training. Morels can be hard to find, something that further adds to their mystique. Asking a friend won't help. Good morel hunting spots are guarded secrets just like any fishing hotspot.

I used to regularly feast on morels back in the '70s while attending college not far from Crooked

Lake. This good fortune was due to a few hours spent attending plant identification and ecology classes, and many hours spent in the woods hunting, fishing and collecting wild edibles. Those old hotspots of my college days no longer exist—gone in the face of forty years of development and changes in forest growth. My morel hunting skills seem to have disappeared with these spots.

With time to kill one present-day misty spring morning, I headed down to the dock with Kaliber in tow, hoping the gods of morel hunting would again smile upon me. Maybe I could find just one morel for a photo shoot. If nothing else, there were plenty of spring flowers to photograph. I fired up the Lund, backed out of the dock, and planed off across the lake to the south bay. The forest there would hold snow-white bunch berries, pale gold bellworts, lavender violets and maybe even a drab tasty morel or two.

I beached the boat alongside a deadfall, tied the anchor rope to an overhanging pine branch, and headed up the steep slope with Kal quartering through the brush ahead. Near the top of the slope I slowed down and started searching the mottled brown and rust leaf litter, scanning for mottled brown and rust cone-shaped morels. I relied on lessons learned many years ago, searching for flat, poorly drained aspen groves with sparse underbrush and a thick cover of last year's leafy mulch. The first morel is the hardest to find. Find one, and more magically appear, not only because of the habitat. Eyes and brain merge and recognize the morel's subtle camouflage.

We moved through the forest, taking pictures, searching for that first mushroom—at least I was. Kal was more interested in the local chipmunk population, and picking up a host of ticks as she loped fifty yards for my ten. I eased down an old logging trail, scanning the jigsaw puzzle of last year's leaves for that one odd, out-of-place piece.

A contradiction in wildflower names, a yellow violet caught my eye at the edge of the trail. I kneeled down, flipped the camera to "macro" and did my best to capture the details of the misty droplets glistening on bright yellow petals. I looked up from the view finder and found a shy morel peeping up from the leaf litter three feet away. I shifted the camera to the mushroom for several shots, gently tipped it loose from the litter, and scanned the area from my knees. A second morel popped into view, growing sidewise from the base of a mossy log.

I may have found a mother lode, a morel honey-hole to visit year after year. I didn't get a chance to find out. Kal, forgotten in my morel hunting trance, suddenly started barking back in the forest with her deep "I got me a critter cornered" voice. My morel treasures were stuffed into a jacket pocket as I hurried over to check out the fuss, hoping it wasn't a bear cub or a skunk.

No angry mother bear or tail-lifting skunk was evident. Kal was dancing around an old stump, barking and pawing at the rotten wood. Expecting no more than a cornered chipmunk, I moved in, only to discover the white-tipped quills of a cowering baby porcupine bristling out of the hollow stump. Encouraged by my courage, Kal lunged in and nipped at the porky through a crack in the side of the stump. She yelped and beat a hasty retreat, with me on her heels. I hurried the dog and her mouthful of quills back to the boat, leaving my morel hotspot behind.

Firewood Happens

Two mushrooms and fifteen porcupine quills don't make for much of a meal. However, the excursion wasn't a total loss. I learned if you want to find the morels, you first need to take time to stop, kneel down, and photograph the flowers. And second, keep the dang dog out of the porcupines.

Hunting Colors

Kaliber and I are supposed to be hunting ducks this morning, alone on Duck Island near the south shore of Crooked Lake. It should be easy to sit back and enjoy my coffee while the intense little retriever whines and quivers with anticipation, watching the duck decoys for suspicious moves. There's just one problem. It's a clear calm morning and the mid-October sun rising through the lake fog is a gold, orange, and pink distraction impossible to ignore.

Those college photography classes that I wasted so much money on many years ago still have their influence. My gun and coffee cup are forgotten for the moment. I dig the cheap little camera out of the backpack and shoot picture after picture of Kal silhouetted against the eastern glow with the trees on Stony Point and the rising, shifting fog as a backdrop.

This trip to the cabin was timed to coincide with peak fall colors. The fog and the sunrise are unexpected bonuses. A ray of sunlight cuts through the drifting haze like a spotlight, illuminating a flame-red maple for just a few seconds, then moving on to dazzle the top of a gold aspen. My mind wanders further from waterfowl hunting as this real life color show changes by the moment. A lone mallard, perhaps the first and last of the day, chooses this moment to appear suddenly out of the fog, flaring back from the decoys, the white undersides of wings flashing in the sun, gone before camera can be traded for shotgun.

Firewood Happens

So few ducks, so many colors. I sling the shotgun over my shoulder, just in case, and take the camera in hand. The dog and I roam the island, hunting autumn colors instead of mallards and wood ducks, armed with 3.2 megapixels, a 6X optical zoom, a 256mb memory card, and a fresh set of batteries. We track down targets of opportunity, shooting at will, looking for different angles as the morning light changes through the drifting fog and mirrors the fall colors on the water.

Each passing minute brings a new photo opportunity. The black Labrador sitting patiently in front of a red dogwood with clusters of ivory berries and a collage of green, gold, orange, and red in the background. The same screen, minus the dog, with a white birch stub providing the contrast. A low, questioning call comes from behind me. Two huge trumpeter swans make a slow mid-level pass down the lake, shining ivory white above the haze. They're too far out for a decent picture. Still, it's a beautiful scene. I shoot three times just to preserve the memory.

We move on, wandering the west side of the island under the overhang of the big white pines. A rose-colored boulder sticks out of the hillside, surrounded by a wealth of gold birch and aspen leaves, highlighted with dull orange pine needles, and covered with patterns of green and gray lichens. The sun beams in on the eastern side of the next island where the beavers have cleared a runway, lighting it with a warm glow. The aspens over my cabin on the far north shore alternate between bright gold and faded yellow depending on the sunlight and mist. There's another ten shots.

It's tempting to rest and bask in the sun, but staying focused on one spot is impossible on a morning like this. We move on to the south side of the island to check for bittersweet vines tangling with the hazelnut and dogwood brush. The hunter-orange bittersweet berries would add new colors to the mix. Marcie has requested that I bring a few lengths of vine back to the cabin. She will shape and tie them together with orange flagging tape, add a few pine cones, and create an expensive-looking holiday wreath for the front of the cabin.

I step past the boulder and turn to take one more shot through the shadows to the sunlit lake. A mad chicken clucking erupts from the pine branch just a few feet above my head. It takes a second too long for my color-addled brain to jolt awake. I try to safely drop the camera and unsling the double barrel in the same fumbling moment. A ruffed grouse explodes from the tree, showering my hat with pine needles as it rockets off through the grove before the gun can be shouldered. It reappears out of range, curving low and fast across the reflections in the still water and out of sight around the corner of the far island.

I stand there a moment, regaining composure, contemplating colors, and visualizing what might have been. Golden brown would have been the color of teriyaki-marinated grouse breast, grilled over red-hot coals, served with a nice white wine and a fresh green salad with bleu cheese dressing. And wondering instead what color of wine goes good with hot dogs.

Winter

Summer—pack a swimsuit, an extra pair of shorts, and maybe a spare t-shirt. Drive north on smooth dry roads and arrive at the cabin with no more worries than how high the grass is or if the loons will yodel. The fridge is stocked, the pantry is full, and it's still light outside. A frosty mug of beer on the deck is the first order of business. That's summer. That's simple.

Now for a winter reality check. On a mid-winter visit, the warm clothes for ice fishing, skiing, and trips to the outhouse take up an entire oversized duffel bag. Marcie and I head north in the dark, on icy roads with the truck packed with clothes and provisions, trusting that neighbor Bill has plowed nine hundred feet of driveway. The pantry shelves will be bare, the fridge unplugged, and any water that was left behind will be frozen as solid as Crooked Lake. That's winter. It's complicated.

First things first—supplies. The last small town is partially open when we arrive, streetlights shining down on deserted streets lined with snow banks —a deserted shell of its bustling summer self. Rib-eye steaks, summer sausage, and double-smoked bacon from the meat market are the first order of business. Then a stop at the combination bait-grocery-gas store down the street. I fill the gas tank while the teenaged store clerk fills a plastic bag with sucker and crappie minnows. You never know, it might be warm enough to fish at sunrise. Marcie grabs a couple of jugs of drinking water, the latest local newspapers, and a hunk of bird suet. We pass on the ninety-centsa-pound green bananas but can't resist the chocolate-covered, Bavarian-cream-filled bakery goodies.

Four miles north of town the road changes from civilized tar to primitive country gravel. The dark forest closes in, a tunnel of snow-cloaked trees creating a Halloween spook house atmosphere. Lucky for us, the driveway is plowed. The single set of narrow tire tracks marring today's dusting of fresh snow confirms that neighbor Marv has made a security check in his old jeep. The truck's headlights swing into the cabin's yard, revealing a maze of more tracks—rabbits, squirrels, and tree-eating deer have been out scrounging in the cold.

Time of arrival is 7 p.m. The thermometer on the snow-covered deck reads a minus ten degrees. The deck gets a quick shoveling so we can open the door and shuffle the first load of supplies and clothes into the cabin. Kal, the big tough hunting dog, cowers in the truck, hiding her sensitive Labrador ears from the low battery squeak of the smoke detectors. Murri, the fluffy white terrier/poodle mix, scampers through the door, eager to find a warm spot. It's a balmy twenty degrees above inside.

While I trek in more supplies and coax Kal from the truck, Marcie cranks the electric space heaters to "High" and huddles up on the couch with a blanket, the little dog, and the newspapers. It's time to catch up with the local news while the heaters do their work. The local police report, always written in a deadpan straight-faced "just the facts, ma'am" style is full of reports of everyday life in the North Country—road-killed deer, cars in the ditch, and fish house robberies. There's also the usual head-scratchers. Why does someone call 911 because people are walking down the road, talking, and wearing glasses? Or report "gun shots heard in the forest" during hunting season?

A couple sheets of crumpled newspaper, dry maple kindling, and a big match yield a roaring fire and serious heat in the wood stove. I sit in front of it, savoring the warmth, still clad in coat, hat, and boots. Kal grabs a stick of kindling and climbs into my lap, littering the floor with chips and splinters while chewing off nervous energy. What's she excited about? Chasing the squirrel horde from the bird feeders in the morning? Fetching sticks in the belly-deep fluff of snow? Or running free, quartering ahead on the lake ice as I ski?

8 p.m.—eleven below outside, twenty-eight above inside. The thermometers indicate an inside warming trend despite the reverse outside. With that established, the outhouse path needs to be shoveled, the door unlocked and the TP situation checked. Sometimes, someone forgets outhouse etiquette and leaves a roll exposed. The resident mouse has his way with it, shredding and scattering pieces in a frenzy of fun. Yes, there is a mouse in the outhouse.

9 p.m.—minus thirteen below outside, forty-five above inside. Even without a thermometer, the forty-five degree threshold is easy to see. The snow tracked in while unloading melts on the stairs and into the rugs. I work magic with the small wood stove, playing the air flow through the damper, watching the flames dance behind the glass door while squeezing out every possible BTU.

10 p.m.—minus sixteen outside, fifty-five above inside. We watch the late news and talk shows, recording temperate readings in the cabin journal to impress summer readers.

11 p.m.—minus seventeen outside, sixty inside. Time to step outside for a last look at the night sky. Sometimes the northern lights play psychedelic tricks, changing colors and shapes while they dance around the

Big Dipper. Other nights Orion blazes on the southern horizon in the midst of a thousand bright stars. Tonight the full moon overrides all these, beaming down from above and ensnaring the cabin in a creepy web of tree branch moon shadows. Down the hill, the lake groans and thumps with the effort of making more ice, adding its own bit of creepy.

Back inside, Kal curls up in her old overstuffed chair, saving energy. She knows there's a long list of tasks to complete tomorrow. Sipping coffee while watching the shadows of the pine-covered islands slide back across the lake towards the sunrise. Pulling on the old snowmobile's starter rope, swearing until it starts. Drilling holes in the lake and hoping the northern pike are hungry. Refilling bird feeders after the squirrels stuff themselves. Hauling firewood from the stacks behind the outhouse. Cross country skiing on the lake. Maybe even a late campfire under the moon and stars at ten below.

While I was out stargazing, Marcie folded down the sofa bed. She's an undefined lump huddled on the far side against the wall, semi-recognizable by the Icelandic wool stocking hat peeking out. It's a scene from a modern day *The Night Before Christmas*. I flip the blankets back to hop in and share some body heat before a long winter's nap. Murri is already there, hidden under the covers and snuggling in my spot. She utters a low protective growl and makes no effort to move. Yes, it's winter, and nothing is simple.

The Rites of
Spring

The Rites of Spring

The arrival of spring is a slow process at Crooked Lake. North-facing hillsides and the forest shade hold white patches long after the frogs begin their spring songs. The driveway is a muddy, treacherous cross-country racecourse that requires four-wheel drive and nerves of steel. The lake ice takes weeks to turn from white to gray to black, lingering until a warm south wind smashes it ashore, tinkling in the waves like broken glass. The smart thing would be to stay away for a few weeks while the seasons work out their differences. But there's work to be done before the crazy days of summer.

The last bundle of wood from the sawmill is still taking up valuable parking space and needs to be chainsawed into firewood-sized pieces. This is good honest work, made easier by the chickadees whistling spring songs in the background. A bit more exciting is the yearly chore of adding new bedding to the wood duck houses. Marcie stands ready with a first aid kid and cell phone while I climb up and cautiously rap on each house. You don't want an excited squirrel, bat, early duck arrival, or wasp colony trying to exit the house via your arm while perched ten feet up on a wobbly ladder.

Even the tedious yard work of raking leaves, piling sticks, and collecting winter-lost litter has its moment. The snow banks that neighbor Bill's old Chevy truck pushed into miniature mountain ranges melt and retreat as stubbornly as the glaciers that covered this land thousands of years ago. Left behind as they shrink is a collection of bits of last year's life, things natural and unnatural, memories, questions, and answers mixed together. A bottle cap from an obscure microbrewery, dropped during a sunny summer afternoon leaning-against-the-truck conversation. A rusty, bent eight-penny nail that may have caused a bloody thumb nail and a few bad words years ago during cabin construction. A faded green tennis ball misplaced by the dogs in the white fluff of New Year's Eve.

Some have more tangible value than others. A single car key, slightly rusty with the manufacturer's logo engraved in plastic and thus solving a mystery. We now know what happened to the car key that Andy has been scratching his head over for months. One other treasure isn't so obvious or valuable in a material sense—a ragged tail feather from the only grouse my friend Neil bagged last October.

Kaliber chased the bird up a hillside and flushed it down the open corridor of a logging trail in front of us. My mind and my camera recorded the scene. Kal, sitting at Neil's feet, looking up at the bird she had just retrieved, knowing she had done well. Neil, holding the bird at arm's length from his orange and brown jacket with a wide smile one would not expect from a stoic farmer.

My musings over junk come to an end as the first chipmunk of the spring rustles through the leaf litter at the edge of the woods. I offer a greeting. "Hey, Chippie, where you been?" It hip hops over to my boot, stops to reward me with its cutest chipmunk pose, and then continues on between my legs towards the all-a-chipmunk-can-eat bird feeder buffet in front of the cabin.

This route passes the corner of the deck where Kal is taking a serious nap, curled up in a green canvas chair after a tough day of squirrel patrol and stick retrieval. She opens one eye and zeros in on the happy little critter hopping through her security zone. The next scene will be repeated uncountable times over the next six months. She scrambles from the chair, sending it, beverage cans, and deck clutter flying, tumbling, clattering, as she launches off the deck in hot pursuit.

Spring has sprung. Let the games begin!

Labrador Spring

I bring matches, firewood, a bucket of water, and a couple of craft-brewed beers to the first campfire of spring. Kaliber brings her favorite stick of the weekend, and her limitless energy. After a 4 a.m. wake-up call and a long day of turkey hunting, I'm content to relax lakeside in a chair, feed the fire, and watch the spring wildlife show. She's ready to play.

Kaliber is the fourth Labrador retriever Marcie and I have raised, all of them black, and all of them female. The first three, Maggie, Brooke, and Ripley, had their personal quirks and their initial puppy energy. They mellowed after two or three years and were content to be companions when hunting season wasn't in season. They asked no more than to be included in whatever was going on, whether it be a walk in the woods, a ride in the boat, or an afternoon on the deck. After all, there's plenty to smell on a walk, plenty to see on a boat ride, and the deck-side bird feeders need to be protected from chipmunks and squirrels—in between naps.

Kal will have none of this. Her grandfather was imported from England, supposedly from the Queen's kennels, and royalty demands attention. An appropriate American term for her would be "High Maintenance." Even at Labrador middle-age, she demands that fun things happen before a nap on the deck. Of course she hunts—pheasants, grouse, ducks, geese, chipmunks, mice —whatever is in season or happens to be available. But Wikipedia, despite its reputation, has her pegged: "As a breed (Labrador retrievers), they are highly intelligent and capable of intense single-mindedness and focus if motivated or their interest is caught."

Intense single-mindedness? No stick is safe with Kal around. She will fetch the same piece of wood for an entire year without losing or tiring of it. She invents games for her own amusement when we tire of her unceasing begging to retrieve. That favorite stick, or maybe a tennis ball or a Frisbee, is carried to the end of the dock and nosed or paw-flipped into the lake. She whines at the sight of her precious toy in peril and then dives in head-first to retrieve. A quick swim back to shore, a water-flinging, ear-flapping shake or two, and repeat over, and over, and over again.

Tonight all the pent-up energy of a late spring, and the disappointment of being left at the cabin while I turkey-hunted, come together. It's as though that intelligent little mind behind the bright amber eyes realizes her springs are counted in people years, not doggie years. She demands to make the most of the handful left to her and pleads with me to play, whining and nudging me with her maple stick.

Crooked Lake calms to a blue sheet of glass in the last hour before dusk, mirroring the green reflections of the pines stepping up the slopes of the islands anchored to the right and left. The beavers, otters, and ducks are busy in a flurry of spring renewal, cutting ripples through the still water in the dim light. Mix in the yodeling loons, with the hooting barred owls, and the occasional coyote choir. Add a lack of man-made sound and it's easy to imagine this same scene playing out every spring for thousands of years.

The dog couldn't care less about all this ambiance. She wants to swim and fetch. I throw the heavy maple stick, sending it twirling down the hill from the campfire time after time, splashing it out into the lake, breaking the smooth surface. She chases, swims, and retrieves, time and time again.

When my arm can take no more, I throw once more. She spins away and chases. "Last one!" I yell after her. She knows what that means, completes the retrieve and presents her precious hunk of maple to me one last time.

"Sweet," I tell her. She crashes back down the bank, ignoring the steps I labored over, and plunges once more into water that was ice only last week. Back and forth, with no particular purpose in mind, she cruises the shore with stick in mouth. The new aluminum roll-in dock is parked on shore but the small wooden one was left in all winter. She occasionally leaves the water, runs to the end of it, does the ritual shake, drops the stick in the water, and dives in head-first to retrieve.

As the evening passes, she checks back at the fire, dripping wet, tail wagging, carrying her stick. "Nice stick," I say. That's all the affirmation she needs. Back down the bank, splash into the lake, and resume swimming. Not a moment of a spring evening is to be wasted, even if I won't be a party to her silly games.

The fire burns down until it's decision time. The smart thing to do would be to tip the water bucket over the coals and make our way up hill to the cabin in the fading light. Tomorrow's predawn turkey hunt wake-up call isn't that far away. But I think I'll open one last beer, put another chunk of oak on the fire, and let this dog have her day. After all, it's spring.

Magic Deer

The third day of deer season is winding down as I make my way into Kittleson's Woods, sneaking down the crooked trail with three hours of light left. The stiff south wind might cover my noise and scent, unless I flush a dang grouse and scare the crap out of me and every deer in this small woodlot.

Kittleson's Woods has not aged well. Windstorms, beavers, disease, and old age have toppled trees, turning this twenty acres into a crisscrossed jungle of aspen, oak, and maple deadfall. Growing up through, around, and intertwined in this natural carnage is world-class prickly ash whose thorny branches clutch, grab, rip, tear, and draw blood through the toughest clothing. My hunting partners and I labored to brush-whack and chainsaw a narrow trail into the center. It ends at the base of a huge old maple tree on the edge of a grassy half-acre swamp.

The tree forks several feet above a four-foot diameter base. The two trunks then reach straight up, almost touching, before branching again and spreading at right angles to form a natural blind. Like most of the trees here, this maple is shedding bark and branches. This might be the last year that common sense allows it to be used as a deer stand. I tie my gun and backpack to a faded green rope and start up the tree using a combination of screw-in steps and the big holes the resident pileated woodpeckers punched into the trunk.

I never have to draw straws with the other guys

for this spot. They think you have to be too patient and quiet to hunt here. If the deer sense an intruder, they bolt out to the west across the farm fields and don't come back. If you reach the tree undetected and wait out the afternoon, there might be the reward of an easy shot at a close deer.

Safe in my perch, leaning back on one big branch and resting my feet on another, I pull up the gun and backpack, and arrange gear and seat cushion. Last of all, a percussion cap is slipped onto the nipple of the muzzleloader, my choice of weapons for the evening. This big 54 caliber rifle was built from a kit over twenty years ago. The barrel and most other metal parts were finished in a modern blue. I stripped off the blue and, with a little trial and error, replaced it with an antique deep brown finish. Then came five coats of oil to the walnut stock, German silver wrist inlays, and a leather sling. The result was the good-looking, serviceable gun now resting across my knees, something an old fur trapper would have carried over one hundred and fifty years ago.

The wind limits sound and visibility for most of the afternoon. I wait until the evening calm arrives with less than an hour of shooting light left. Now is the time to be super still and super silent. Time to settle deep into my parka to fend off the chill and try to move only eyes, peering across the swamp into the glare and shadows of the late afternoon sun. The stillness brings out the chickadees, nuthatches, and woodpeckers that love these woods. A grouse wanders down the trail, making just enough noise to get my heart thumping. Why are these birds so plentiful and stupid when I am carrying a deer rifle, and so scarce and smart when a shotgun is handy?

I don't often see or hear deer that are relaxed and shuffling through the leaves towards me. Most simply appear out of nowhere, standing on the opposite side of the swamp or down to the left where the trail bends to the south. I should be used to these tricks. Again this evening I wonder if the deer in this thicket possess a magical ability to change and move about as silent, invisible ghosts.

With only minutes of fading light left, a deer is standing, head up, in the tall grass of the swamp, fifteen yards away. My heart races from stupor to high speed and adrenaline hits like an electric shock. I don't believe my eyes in the gathering gloom and close them to clear my vision. When they reopen, the shadows and light were playing tricks on my aging sight. The "deer" is now a headless log horizontal in the swamp grass.

I relax and inwardly laugh at myself. The suspense of deer hunting can still make me see things, even after more than forty years of experience. My heart rate has almost returned to normal when the "log" raises its head from the grass and this time clearly establishes itself as a deer spitting distance away.

It is no trophy buck. It is a fat young doe, a prime candidate for the empty space in my freezer. My heart speeds up again as I slowly, carefully, cock the hammer to avoid a loud telltale click. The muzzle moves a few inches to settle the sights behind the deer's shoulder. My finger tightens on the front trigger. The muzzleloader roars, rocks me back, and blocks the scene with the gray smoke and orange muzzle flash of 110 grains of old-fashioned black powder.

As the smoke clears and the echoes die out, I

settle back onto my perch and wait. There is no need to hurry. The deer disappeared into the dim light and thickness of the woods. But my ears tracked its sprint through the brush west and the final loud crash as it went down hard. The round lead ball stole its magic.

I'll climb down from the tree in a few minutes and get to work. Kittleson's Woods doesn't give up deer easily. The drag in the dark through the prickly ash, and over the deadfalls won't be pleasant and will give me a reason to complain—until my return next year. What sort of crazy magic spell have these woods cast over me?

Fresh Fish on Ice

Dale and I busted the portable fish house loose from its unproductive location and slid it across the frozen, snow-covered surface of Crooked Lake. Packed inside the house were fishing rods, tackle boxes, ice auger, fish finder, heater, snacks, beer—everything needed by the modern ice fisherman to bag a limit. And we had better get some. Our wives, sisters, practically twins, had issued an ultimatum—"Bring back fish or go hungry!"

Crooked Lake, with its steep shores and snow-covered ice, is not an easy place to fish in the winter, especially for the fish Cris and Marcie were demanding. Crappies, fried to crispy deliciousness, minutes from the clear, cold water. Tonight might be different. We had insider information. Neighbor Marv had confirmed that crappies were biting after dark "by the white birch clump." Better yet, he offered a Minnesota Nice invitation to move over and share his good fortune. We drilled holes near his faded green canvas house and were ready when Marv zoomed up on his snowmobile.

Marv retired a year or two ago and took up ice fishing to pass away the long winter days and nights. He acquired a snowmobile, fish house, and ice auger in rapid succession. However, his retirement funds were not squandered frivolously. The snowmobile was new—twenty-five years ago. The fish house was a genuine Sears Roebuck of about the same vintage. The ice auger? A garage sale special that needed some carburetor work, if I remember right. Add a few old jiggle stick fishing rods with heavy black line and you can picture Marv as an ice fishing extra on the set of *Grumpy Old Men.*

Marv was quick to offer advice. "I've been getting them about eight feet down right when it starts to get dark. I had five nice ones last night." Dale and I kept our thoughts to ourselves. If Marv could catch five "nice ones" with his archaic equipment, we should have no trouble bagging enough for a fish fry and prove a little something to him and our wives in the process.

We wished him good luck and tucked into our high tech hideout. The heater warmed the cozy space just enough to keep the holes open. Squirming minnows dipped from the bait bucket were hooked and suspended under black and gold bobbers in two holes. Glow-in-the-dark jigs tipped with lively minnows went down two more. We waited as the sun sank towards the western shore, the fish finder's lighted dial promising twelve feet of water, but no fish. That changed right at sundown when the electronic gizmo began flashing yellow bars at eight feet. The hungry crappies had arrived.

The next half hour of bedlam was pure revenge, payback for the many days we spent fishless and freezing on this same lake. A rod tip would bob, arc with the hook set, and yield its black and silver crappie reward. A bobber would twitch, slowly sink, the rod would be grabbed and held between knees while still dealing with the first one. Beers were knocked over and forgotten. A metal ice scoop slid across the floor and down a hole, lost forever in the watery depths. Fish unhooked themselves, flopped across the icy floor, and escaped down other holes. We didn't care. There were more where those came from.

Most of the crappies were small and sent back down the holes. Some were big enough to be judged "keepers" and flipped into a waiting bucket. A fish fry and happy wives were in our future. The action was still hot when we heard Marv crunch through the snow to us. He unzipped the door and poked his head in. "How you guys doing? I've got a half dozen."

"Not bad. We must have at least ten," I said, smugly holding up the current modest, still wiggling victim.

Marv sized it up, then shined his flashlight down into our fish bucket. He picked one out and held it up to the light. "Oh, I didn't know you were keeping small ones."

I glanced over at Dale and tried to compose an answer. "Ah, well, the wives want to have a fish fry . . . "

"I'll give you mine—that should help." Marv disappeared, crunching away into the dark for a minute, and then reappearing. "Here you go."

He dumped six "definitely keeper" crappies in on top of our shrinking prizes. "Say hi to Cris and Marcie for me. I'll stop over later for a drink."

We fished on, a bit more humble, and added a few more "maybes" to the bucket before the bite slowed and the lure of the warm cabin, food, and drink pulled us.

The cold of a well-below-zero January night shocked our lungs as we unzipped the door and stepped outside. The walk back to shore in the moonless night was a classic home-coming scene. Our boots crunching and squeaking on the light snow cover. The lake cracking and booming underneath us, making new ice.

Our head lamps sending shafts of light ahead through the darkness, clouded with the fog of our breath. Above us the stars sparkled—a million precious diamonds just out of reach in an ink black sky. The warm lights of the cabin ahead, welcoming us through the trees with a hint of wood smoke wafting down the hill.

We paused at the lake shore to savor the moment. "I'll clean fish while you set up the fryer," I offered to Dale. "We're going to be heroes with the wives!"

"Yeah," he replied, looking up the slope to the cabin lights. "At least as long as Marv keeps his mouth shut."

Last Day Mystery

The fog-bound shores of Crooked Lake echoed with strange cries just before sunrise. "Puck, Puck, Puck, Aaaammaaaaggg, Puck, Puck, Aaamaaaagggg." Forty-five years of duck hunting experience and a degree in Biology were no help in identifying this crazy noise. I huddled alone in my island duck blind, shivering in the damp cold of a November dawn, wondering what mystery creature the sun would reveal.

Crooked Lake is usually iced over by mid-November. Open water wasn't anticipated when I stopped for a quick visit on the way home from deer camp. But there it was and, with it, the opportunity for one last duck hunt, even though my faithful retriever wasn't along. Dogs aren't allowed at deer camp. She was home pouting and driving Marcie crazy.

An hour before sunrise I had motored across the dark lake with Orion for a guide, standing out brighter than the other stars of the southern sky. A patch of skim ice surprised me halfway across. The boat cut through, crunching and clanging like an arctic ice breaker. Once free of that unexpected hazard, the water on the eastern point of Duck Island was still ice free and ready to accommodate a motley batch of duck decoys. Breakfast was a granola bar, a cup of coffee and a slow sunrise, waiting for the light, listening for wings cutting through the still air above.

They started well before shooting time. Small flocks, and ones and twos, winging down the main lake to the left and over the narrow channel on the right. Heard, but not seen, whistling past the point in the dark and skidding down far out in the open water. I waited, anticipating a sunrise that would bring ducks wheeling through the decoys and an answer to mystery cries building as sunrise approached. Then the fog rolled in, blotting out the dawn, turning the lake to a murky pool of silver shimmering in what little light fought through the gloom.

The suspense grew as a pair of goldeneye ducks swam out of the fog, appearing at the far edge of the decoys without a sound. They eyed the fake ducks, turning heads, cruising at extreme shotgun range. Flushing them for a shot would be a chancy thing. The lake would come alive with spooked ducks disappearing into the fog, taking the unknown noise makers with them.

The sun rolled back the shroud of fog bit by bit, opening the curtain on daylight and revealing the mystery. Crooked Lake was hosting a hooded merganser convention—small, fish-eating, diving ducks that are normally quiet except for an occasional squawk. In this case, the drakes were feeling feisty and looking to impress potential mates.

Small family groups of drab white/brown/gray hens and juveniles were scattered around the lake, diving, splashing, and feeding on the fall bounty of young fish and minnows. Fewer drakes were mixed in, dressed in formal black and white tuxedo plumage, busy practicing complex mating rituals among the oblivious hens. A drake would rise up in the water, fluff a white-feathered head crest, throw back a long narrow bill, and shout out "Puck, Puck, Aaaammmmoooog" to the world. Others would answer back, repeating this primeval cry up and down the lake.

Since fish-eating mergansers rank low as table fare, I was content to enjoy the silliness of the love-struck mergansers and hope that the lake full of live decoys would draw in more desirable waterfowl. Patience was rewarded with the telltale whistle of goldeneye wings.

A flock of eight curved around the island and dove towards the decoys. I flock shot with the first barrel, missing like I always do, waited until they cleared the pine tree in front of the blind, and shot once more. A hen slanted down from the flock, sailed for a moment on set wings, crashing down hard far out in the lake. I scooped the shells out of the gun, reloaded, and watched the bedlam as the gunfire echoed across the water.

Hundreds of mergansers erupted from the lake, wings and feet beating once-still water, lifting off and circling the pine-covered shores. Mergansers crisscrossed the sky and zoomed past both sides of the island. Colorful drakes splashed down briefly in the decoys and then took flight again, paddling the surface as they strained to make lift-off speed. Brown hens wheeled in and flared in my face, white bellies almost close enough to touch. I remained in the blind with the gun on safe, content to be a spectator.

The flurry of activity gradually tapered off as the mergansers moved their convention to the next lake. Another half hour brought no more ducks while the sunrise continued on a perfect late autumn day. I retrieved the boat from hiding and took my time picking up decoys, savoring this last hunt, this last morning on the water. First came the single fake bluebills. Then the prized sleeper decoys strung two by two, next the mallards and the goose. The two shared strings of five bluebills were saved for last, stacked to avoid line tangles. Maybe one of my sons or a nephew could get here for a last hunt of their own. Then it was time to start the motor and go looking for the goldeneye, drifting somewhere with the breeze along the shore of a far island.

I rounded a point and flushed a dull brown immature eagle and two ravens from an overhanging pine. A quick accusation came to mind—the hungry young eagle and his raven buddies had just made a meal out my duck. But the eagle had waited too long, no doubt with the ravens egging him, to feast on fresh goldeneye this morning. The duck was floating in the lake, just off shore of the tree.

I motored over, scooped the duck into the boat, and took time to admire the orange and brown legs, dull rust head, and white belly with water drops clinging to downy feathers. Some hunters would complain about a slow morning shoot and a single drab hen goldeneye. I wouldn't agree. The gods of duck hunting had allowed me one last day in the island blind while witnessing a true life nature drama. And a duck had been bagged and rescued from an eagle and his raven entourage. That's no ordinary morning.

Deer the Hard way

The automatic coffee maker gurgled to life an hour before dawn, a wake-up call to a chilly cabin. I rekindled the fire in the wood burner and checked the outdoor temperature. Twenty-seven degrees below zero. If that wasn't enough bad news, a stiff northwest breeze was piling on negative double digits in wind chill. The sunrise on the last day of the muzzleloader deer season was watched from the comfort of the cabin, coffee cup in hand, warm.

The temperature hit ten below at 10 a.m. with boredom setting in. It was time for one last foray into the forest. I bundled up in my warmest ice fishing clothes, layered them with hunter orange, and stepped outside to load the gun. First two percussion caps were fired through the empty muzzleloader, clearing the ignition channel. Next, 110 grains of old fashioned black powder and a big 54 caliber Maxi-Ball bullet were sent down the barrel and seated with a firm push of the ramrod. The nipple was recapped with a percussion cap and the hammer eased down. Ready at last, I headed down the hill to frozen Crooked Lake.

Muzzleloader hunting has gone through major changes in the years since the walnut-stocked and rust-browned gun in my hands was assembled from a mail-order kit. Among these changes are more deer, more hunters, heated insulated deer stands, and managed food plots. The guns have also changed. The vast majority of late muzzleloader season hunters now carry guns with modernized in-line ignition systems, utilizing shotgun shell primers to ignite clean burning powder formulations that zip plastic-wrapped bullets down the barrel. There's even a battery-powered electronic-ignition rifle if that's what flips your switch.

There are still a few of us that are willing to forego these "improvements." We would rather wander the forest, looking for the challenge of hunting deer thinned-out and wary from the regular firearm season, with guns that would have been in fashion one hundred and fifty or two hundred years ago. Why? Probably for the same reasons many outdoorsmen and women choose to fly fish with handtied feather bug imitations or to paddle and portage into the Boundary Waters Canoe Area Wilderness. Not every outdoor experience needs to be easy to be enjoyed.

This was the fourth day at the cabin. Cold weather had moved in behind fresh snow, pushing the temperatures farther below zero each morning. The nasty weather had its advantages. The cold kept other hunters in their warm houses and trucks. Road hunters had been my only competition across thousands of acres of state forest. The fresh snow also helped pin-point where deer were hanging out in the thick overgrown clear cuts and swamps.

That didn't make hunting easy. The snow squeaked and crunched beneath insulated boots, announcing my intrusions into the forest. The cold left two choices for tactics. Either bundle up to the point of immobility and find a comfortable stump for a seat, or dress light and keep moving for warmth. Most of the time I chose to be mobile, squeaking and crunching through the woods, hoping my quarry would make a fatal mistake.

The deer refused to cooperate. They bounded from daytime beds and beat hasty retreats, crashing away through thick pine plantations and bamboo-like aspen thickets. They snorted from distant ridges, mocking me and warning their comrades. They slunk away silent, alerted by grouse exploding out of the snow at my feet.

On this final morning, I crossed the ice to a pine tree-studded shore, feeling the cold bite of the wind funneling down the gap between it and Big Island. Behind the steep banks is a pothole- and swamp-dotted chunk of forest. Deer use it as a daytime refuge, heading out to raid tree plantations and lake home bird feeders under the cover of darkness. Maybe, just maybe, one would get restless in the cold and wander from its bed for a midday snack.

I scaled the brushy hillside, boots squeaking, towards a narrow ridge splitting an upland bog from the lake. Right on cue, a grouse flushed from the snow, scared the crap out of me, and rattled off through the snow-frocked aspens, leaving a trail of powder hanging behind in the cold air. I overcame that little surprise and continued on to the top of the ridge and a seat on a deadfall.

It was a cold place to sit, despite the sun beaming down through the pines. The wind leaked through, creeping layer by layer past my high-tech clothes. I lasted an hour and a half, scanning the slopes while juggling hand warmers in gloves, looking for any small movement to distract attention from numbing nose and toes. The warm comfort of the cabin and the excuse of packing for the trip home beckoned.

I slung my pack, picked up the gun, and began traversing the slope down to the lake, trying to prevent a slip and a wild toboggan ride down and out onto the ice. Ten feet above the lake, I paused to consider the next move while mentally noting the fresh deer tracks paralleling the bank.

It was then that a semi-frozen brain called my attention to a deer, out on the ice, trotting down the shore. The next series of events unfolded in slow motion, courtesy of the subzero temperatures and my cold thick blood. I fumbled with the gun's hammer, pulled it back, and poked a numb, glove-clad finger through the trigger guard. The deer stopped forty yards down the shore and lifted its head to browse a white pine branch. I lined up the open sights, pulled the trigger, and was rewarded by the boom of the gun—flat, subdued and hollow in the thick air.

A few moments later, I was kneeling on the ice of Crooked Lake, admiring the luxurious thick hair of a winter northern Minnesota whitetail. It was a young doe, cleanly harvested on the last day of the season, at ten degrees below zero, with a gun Davy Crockett would have been proud of. Not a wide-racked buck. Not what most hunters would call a trophy. Not an easy deer.

The Order of the
Evening

The Order of the Evening

Life is not always simple, even at the lake, even at our small cabin. What seems an improvement or upgrade, something meant to make life easier, can have unintended consequences. For example, consider that the addition of electricity has proved both a blessing and a curse. Whether cooking, reading or writing, long winter nights are now brighter and tolerable within the vaulted ceiling of its well-lit one room. Now for the curse—television.

We didn't have a TV in the beginning, before electricity, since there was only kerosene, gas, or hand power. Now, as the light fades early on dreary winter afternoons, a person can retreat to the cozy confines of the cabin, throw another log in the wood burner, and turn on the television. There, on the one, sometimes two available channels, is the latest bad news. Terrorist attacks, drug wars, and "forensic" detective shows have made their bloody, noisy arrival. With them comes the sense that the world, perhaps the universe, is badly out of order even here in the woods.

So let's forget those dark winter months and the bright lights of the flat screen. It's April now. The lake has shed the bonds of two feet of ice and the soft glow of a spring evening is upon us. We have natural outdoor light late into the evening and time to enjoy it. Food is the first order of business, supper out on the deck. The white-hot coals in the grill char three rib-eye steaks and a loaf of artisan bread. Add a salad, a bottle of wine, and Marcie, my sister Sharon, and I have a quick simple supper with minimal cleanup.

Another bottle of wine makes its way down the hill to the lakeside campfire ring. Evening calm is settling across the lake under a clear sky. The islands anchored out in front cast mirrored reflections on the water as we build the fire and relax into the Adirondack chairs. Kaliber amuses herself on the dock, peering down into the water, hoping the summer sunfish will come out and play. A pair of loons cruises down the shore to investigate while a blue heron lumbers across the water, squawking like a million-year-old pterodactyl.

Our quiet conversation does nothing to disturb the activity around us. The resident wood ducks are back from down south and busy checking out nesting boxes. A pair flies into an aspen tree halfway up the hill. The drab gray hen hops down to the roof of a nest box and bends her head into the entrance, inspecting the interior and the fresh cedar shavings I packed inside last month. The drake waits like a well-dressed prom date, all decked out in spring courting plumage. They fly off up the hill through the aspens, maybe not impressed with the location.

Right on time, just before dark, the barred owls in the old pines on Big Island proclaim their dominance. The loud rhythmic hoots echo back across the lake and touch off a second round. I answer back just for fun—"Whoooo cooks for you! Whoooo cooks for youoooooooo!" in a weak attempt to entice one across the channel. This trick doesn't work often. When it does, the owl sneaks in on soundless wings, booms a challenge from a close perch, and scares the hell out of everyone. The owl passes on that fun tonight.

The hooting does rile up the neighborhood coyote packs. A bark, a yip, then a full-scale howling chorus erupts from the southern group on the far side of the lake. Not to be outdone, the northern pack, half a mile behind us in the forest, joins in. We listen in silence, the hair on the backs of our necks at attention in a primal response, a reminder of just how alive we are after the long winter.

The background bedlam of the spring frog songs rises as the daylight fades. Time to feed more wood to the fire and enjoy the half-moon beaming down through the pine branches. Kal paces on the dock and barks out over the lake, sending more echoes bouncing back from Big Island. An arrowhead of ripples cuts through the still bay. The cruising beaver slaps its tail in defiance and dares Kal to jump in. I call out a reprimand and she joins us at the fire, willing to forego a wrestling match with a beaver in icy water.

The activity fades with the light. Marcie and Sharon decide that they've had enough excitement for the night and take their leave from the fire. Kal and I linger, watch the beam of their flashlight weave up the trail to the dark cabin, and turn back to the lake. The beaver cruising in front of the dock continues to fascinate the dog. Her outline, sil-houetted by the sparking firelight against the dark blue lake, is a study in intense concentration.

The coyotes can't resist one more round of howling at the moon. Both packs tune up and try to outdo each other. Kal listens, head tilted, the beaver forgotten for the moment. I wonder what's going through her doggie mind. Uneasiness? An urge to join in the howling? Disdain for these wild relatives given her royal English bloodlines? I wait for the serenade to die out before taking the handle of the orange water bucket and tipping it to drown the fire. The morning sun will bring forth a new spring day, one to be rested and ready for.

Kal and I stumble up the trail towards the cabin. The lack of a flashlight and the lateness of the night seem to have affected my coordination. Or could it be the wine? Halfway up the hill, the loons bring us to a stop. It begins as a faint yodel from the far southern bay. Our local loons are quick to answer back, louder, closer and with more notes. East Bay and West Bay pairs weigh in at full volume and absolute craziness breaks out across the water as these northwoods icons live up to their names. The echoes of the crazy laughter gradually die out and once again the frog songs well up in the background.

Ahead through the trees, the light of the TV is flickering in the cabin windows, no doubt tuned to the late news and again spreading rumors and gossip of all sorts of bad things. Maybe I'll just pull up a chair on the deck and listen to the frogs for a while. Out here, in the dim light of a northern spring evening, with the dog at my feet, everything seems to be in order.

Deck Time

I knew that building the cabin would be a complicated, time-consuming learning experience. Budgets, materials, and schedules are natural issues on construction projects. These are bound to be multiplied when the labor force consists of yourself and whatever friends and relatives can be coerced into giving up some of their own valuable time. What I didn't expect was that the cabin would be a work-in-progress over ten years from the start. In hindsight, a critical mistake was made early in the project. I added a deck to the front of the cabin.

Every cabin should have a deck, patio, or similar defined outdoor area. Without one, the cabin may be useable but not complete. However, the timing of the deck construction can be critical to the completion of the rest of the cabin. The most important advice I can offer to other do-it-yourself cabin builders is to not, under any circumstances, build the deck until the cabin is finished or at least livable.

In my defense, this deck was built out of necessity. Providing a front step that was safer and had more curb appeal than a stack of wood pallets had my modest carpentry skills baffled. A deck on the front, the non-lake side, wasn't in our original plans since the lake was the focus of the building site. It happened because I knew how to build a deck, the expense was not so much, and we needed those steps. The critical mistake was failing to recognize what a distraction it would be to the rest of the cabin project, even without a view of the lake.

Marcie bought a couple of canvas folding chairs as temporary furniture the minute the deck was usable. I wish she would have got the small cheap ones instead of the sturdy over-sized chairs with the double cup holders. Their comfortable confines have proven to be more inviting than manual labor like siding and shingling, especially when there is a beverage or two in the double cup holders. Add a helpful friend with a cooler full of snacks, and progress on the cabin can grind to a halt.

I also discovered that our dogs love decks, especially if they get a chair of their own. The deck is a perfect spot to lie in ambush for bird feeder-raiding chipmunks and squirrels. It also provides an elevated platform to leap off of in pursuit of tennis balls, sticks, or any other thrown object. Thus a deck, a dog, and a tennis ball can provide hours of entertainment while the building projects continue to suffer. On the positive side, my hammer-swinging arm gets plenty of exercise and stays limber throwing things for the mutts, just in case I find the time to tackle a project.

One other related deck distraction is worth mentioning. Bird feeders, more accurately called chipmunk and squirrel feeders, are another necessity at a cabin. Birdseed should be a legitimate itemized expense on any cabin owner's taxes. Again, be careful. Bird-watching from the deck can turn into a time-killing distraction. Especially if you add hummingbird feeders like we did. Now cute hummingbirds buzz the deck during the best four working months of the year.

I can't say that hanging out on the deck has

been a total waste of time. I have picked up some important and interesting knowledge. Like how fierce and territorial male hummingbirds are, guarding feeders with iridescent ruby and emerald colors flashing, vocalizing displeasure at their kin in angry munchkin twittering. And that a chipmunk can stuff his cheek pouches to bursting with birdseed and still be light enough on his four little feet to escape the charge of a Labrador retriever. I can also tell which of my wood duck houses are occupied due to hours of patient observation from the comfort of my chair.

The biggest problem is how easy it is to lean back, put my feet up on the short railing, and take a summer nap in the shade with a dog at my feet. I fear that one day I will awaken from a Rip Van Winkle deck nap and find the aspen leaves of autumn falling around me, swirling like a blizzard of golden snowflakes. But unlike Rip Van Winkle, nothing in my world will have changed. The outhouse roof will still be leaking and the firewood won't be stacked. A summer's worth of undone cabin projects will still be waiting.

My Northwoods
Persona

I hurried into the small town lumberyard while Andy and Kaliber waited in the pickup. A couple extra 4x4 posts for our annual Labor Day trip to the farm and we'd be back on the road. But things don't move too fast in small town lumberyards, especially on late summer Saturday mornings. A middle-aged couple was ahead of me at the cash register, taking their time, making small talk with the clerk while settling up on some trim for the final touches on their home addition.

I willed myself to slow down and killed some time checking out the paneling samples displayed on the south wall while mentally checking a list of the supplies already packed in the truck. The couple finished up and headed out the door, leaving the harried baseball-capped clerk to deal with me.

"I just need a couple treated 4x4s—twelve footers if you got them," I told him.

"Man, I don't know," he said, tapping the keys on the computer register, checking inventory. "We're getting a new shipment in next week. I know we have a few left but they're pretty scabby." He looked up, expecting trouble.

"No problem," I replied. "This is deer stand material. I don't need the good stuff when I'm doing chainsaw architecture."

That made him happy. "Great! These should work. We were going to throw together a pile of deer stand material next week—I'll discount them. I love people like you!"

I heard a quiet laugh behind me and looked over

my shoulder to see a new customer had arrived and was grinning at the conversation. This guy looked like he knew a thing or two about chainsaws and deer stands. All six-and-a-half feet and at least two hundred and fifty pounds of him were clothed in a mixture of shoulder-length gray hair, a half-buttoned flannel shirt, and a pair of bib overalls with a patina of grease and grime. In spite of this rough look, my first impression was that he probably had a part-time job as Santa Claus during the holiday season. Harmless, quiet, and friendly were words that came to mind.

I smiled back, paid up, and walked out, chuckling to myself at the note printed on the bottom of the invoice—"UGLY!!!!! Deer stand material!!!!"

Andy was waiting in the truck, ready with a comment. "Did you meet Paul Bunyan?"

He was right. The cheerful giant now being waited on in the store could have been the great grandson of Paul Bunyan. But there was more. Andy pointed to the right. "Look at his truck."

There, without question, sat the modern day version of Babe the Blue Ox. The 1980ish Ford flatbed had the look of a vehicle that has a name. Babe would do fine, even if green and rust weren't the correct colors. No fuzzy dice or wedding garters hung from the rear-view mirror. Spare chainsaw chains were the interior décor of this old girl. And while Babe the Blue Ox may have pulled a cart loaded with handsaw, pike, and lunch box, the bed of this truck was piled with gas cans, a couple beat-up chainsaws, and a mostly empty twelve pack of Bud Lite.

I couldn't help but feel a bit jealous as we loaded the crooked posts and headed on down the road. I had a better truck, a good companion in my oldest son, and a well-bred dog with her head sticking between us from the back, eager for the adventure ahead. But this guy, perhaps ten or fifteen years younger than I, was a guy that had his life figured out. I'm willing to bet everyone in town knew of the big guy that drove that old truck—he was someone you noticed and remembered.

Maybe it came easy to him. Perhaps, unlike me, he was born here and had his path in life laid out by birthright. He just did what came naturally. In contrast, here I was, well over half a century old, unnoticed, and struggling with my image and identity.

I don't have the wardrobe, the money, or the fancy log cabin needed to be the "Rich Guy from the Cities." Unless I win the lottery, that's not going to happen. I have thought about trying the "quirky environmentalist with the long hair and ponytail" thing. After all, I used to have long hair and "Environmentalist" has been part of my job title for over thirty years. However, Marcie would probably nix the long hair even though I had it when we first met. I also don't have the build or the equipment to pull off the Paul Bunyan logger look like the guy back at the lumberyard. And Marcie would not go for the bib overalls look either, even though she used to wear them back in those college days.

These thoughts kept with me through our day of deer stand building at the farm and into the next morning back at the cabin. While everyone else snoozed the morning away, the dog and I wandered down to the dock and fired up the little boat. Late summer is not the best time to fish Crooked Lake. The crappies have long since left the shallows, chased out by hordes of bait-stealing, stunted sunfish. The bigger northern pike have likewise retreated to depths unknown. It didn't matter today. A full mug of coffee, a fishing rod, a boat, and a dog make a good combination on a lazy summer morning. There's always hope when you are fishing.

We headed east down the shore, idling along just outside of the oval-leafed pondweeds marking the edge of the shallows. A king fisher chattered, dropped from the overhanging branch of a dead oak and flew up the shore to the next branch. We caught up and it repeated the process, leapfrogging ahead down the shore of Bird Island, one branch at a time. I cut the motor at the south tip of the island and drifted across to Stony Point, casting a surface lure to the lily pads. A bass smacked the lure from below and dove deep into the weeds, freeing itself almost immediately. After that quick excitement, there was nothing more than a silly hammer-handle-sized northern pike that took a run at the frog-colored lure sputtering through the lilies and arched out of the water like a dolphin, missing it and making me laugh out loud.

Kal and I continued on, trolling a loop around our bay. Only one other boat was visible, a classic red and white Lund like mine, drifting along Big Island. I didn't recognize the boat or the lone angler that sat in the stern, casting towards shore with a push-button reel. I cut the motor and waved while Kal stood on the gunwale, tail wagging, eager to meet a new friend. "How's fishing?" I called over.

An elderly man, well into his seventies, or maybe even eighty-something, smiled back out the hood of his sweatshirt. "Oh, not too bad. Haven't caught anything but I had a couple nice bass on."

"Same with me—lost a nice one in the weeds back there by the point."

"Well, that's fishing," he replied. "I don't really care. It's just nice being out here—it's a beautiful morning on a beautiful lake. Too bad I have to head home soon. Take care!"

I waved a farewell, restarted the motor and trolled away, finishing the lap around the bay before coasting in to the dock. We started up the stairs to the cabin and stopped for a last look at the lake, just in time to see the old guy motor out from behind the island, aiming back towards the boat access. A stereotype came to mind. Parked back at the access was a ten-year-old pickup, shiny, clean, and looking like it just rolled off the showroom floor. Somewhere back in town, in a cozy well-kept home, was a gray-haired grandmother, making coffee and baking cookies, waiting for her husband to return from the morning's outing.

Kal wagged her tail, watching like an old friend was leaving and she wished he would come back. That's when it dawned that I might have just seen the future, me a quarter of a century from now. Not a well-dressed rich guy with a fancy boat. Not an old hippy environmental activist with long gray hair pulled back in a ponytail. Not an aged Paul Bunyan wannabe in bibs. Just some quiet old guy, happy to be fishing on one more summer day.

So, maybe that's the future. And maybe that's not so bad. But I wonder, maybe, if I could have a black dog riding in the boat with me?

Leaving?

When I brag about our humble cabin, as I often do, it's not unusual to hear negative feedback. Not everyone shares my dream of a lake cabin in the northwoods. Some have tried and discarded that dream. Yard and cabin maintenance lead the list of reasons —"It was just another lawn to mow and another house to paint." Time and taxes are also common laments. "We used to have a cabin but we never had time to use it. We got tired of paying the taxes." There is some truth to these complaints. Owning a simple recreational cabin or a grand lake home is another commitment, another property to maintain, one more worry in a hectic, trouble-filled world, and more than just one more bill to pay.

Some of us have always been willing to look past these negatives even though we may question our sanity and commitment on occasion. At least for me, time at the cabin is better spent than years of weekly visits to the shrink's office. I'm willing to bet the cabin has added years to my life.

Our five acres on the edge of the state forest sounds like paradise when I start talking. No hard-sell sales pitch from a Realtor was needed. Had there been one, it would have read like this—"Eagles, loons, ospreys, bears (maybe not), otters and deer. Heavily wooded hillsides, magnificent lake views, and mature Norway pines standing stately on two hundred feet of frontage on a Natural Environment Lake. Enjoy the seclusion. Build your dream lodge or family retreat on five acres at the edge of thousands of acres of state forest."

Any smart Realtor would have stayed away from mentioning a few other details. Included, free of charge, were industrial-strength poison ivy, mosquitoes, black flies, deer flies, horse flies, and two types of blood-sucking disease-carrying ticks. The property does not have, and will never have, a gentle slope to the lake or a picture-perfect sand beach. Many friends and family were not impressed on their first visit. They were smart enough to recognize that I would be leaning on their strong backs and weak minds for some of the nasty physical labor needed for road clearing, campsite development and, eventually, cabin construction.

All these issues might have driven me nuts if it hadn't been for the dock, one of my first projects. I didn't have a psychiatric need in mind. The kids, dog, Marcie, and I just wanted to be ready to enjoy the first summer at the lake. The dock sections were constructed in my home garage during the winter in anticipation of getting the dock in right after ice-out. Not wanting to be called cheap or lazy, the plans called for a wide sturdy dock built of 8x4 sections of treated rot-proof lumber. The first section was a fast and easy project—until I tried to move it to a corner of the garage. Let's say that section was a little heavy. The plans were revised to call for a three-foot-wide dock.

The first test of my commitment to the cabin dream came on a late June weekend the first summer we owned the land. I arrived on Friday evening after a four-hour drive in my old truck with Ripley the Retriever for company. The weekend was to be spent on manual labor such as building an outhouse and clearing brush for a fire ring and campsite with a little fishing thrown in for variety.

But like my dock plans, things didn't work out that way. The entire weekend was spent wrestling with balky chainsaws, broken shovels, and the aggravation of not having the right tool for whatever job I tackled. While the only real casualty was a gas can crushed flat by a dead birch that fell the wrong way when a chainsaw did work, I accomplished almost nothing. Assisting in building my frustration level were the bugs. The deer flies nearly ate us alive during the day and the mosquitoes made the nightly campfire a battle to maintain a normal body fluid level. And did I mention the heat and humidity? The lack of a cool breeze? Or the fish that didn't bite?

I admitted defeat at noon on Sunday and packed the old truck. I trudged down the hill to the lake with the dog at my heels, hot, exhausted, and frustrated, and escorted by a halo of buzzing deer flies. At least Ripley and I could go for a final swim and cool off for the trip home in the non-air-conditioned truck. We swam for a while and then retired to the dock. There I sat, cooler now, still flailing at deer flies and contemplating the situation, questioning the wisdom of squandering time, efforts, and money to turn this jungle into a paradise.

Then the lake and the dock started to work their magic. I relaxed, teased the resident sunfish with dead deer flies, and wasted more time. A commotion in the water in the channel between the big island and the main shore caught my attention. Two otters were at play—tussling, diving, chirping, and splashing down the lake towards me. Watching otters play is like watching a litter of puppies in a backyard or a kindergarten class playground at recess. You're going to smile. They were oblivious to our presence, wrestling in and out of the weeds and fallen trees along shore. For them, life was good on Crooked Lake.

They were only feet away when they spotted me sitting on the dock, holding back the dog. Both half rose out of the water, forearms bent, eyeing us like suspicious, furry little mermaids. One scolded us with a loud "CHUFF." Then they continued down the shore, more interested in play than us.

I walked back up the hill with the dripping wet dog, much cooler and reenergized. The climb seemed shorter and not as steep. A cool breeze was coming off the lake and the bugs were gone. Maybe I just imagined all that change. Then again, maybe a loon even called a lonesome farewell in the background. I drove off much happier, no longer doubting my commitment.

So take note if you are thinking about starting or ending cabin life. Those same doubts about time, commitment, and money will cross your mind, sooner than later, just as they did mine that summer day. When it happens, here's some more cheap advice.

Never leave the cabin without taking a time out. If summer be the season, head to the dock. Let the sunfish nibble your toes while you watch the dragonflies chase mosquitoes. Maybe an osprey, an eagle, or a turkey buzzard will catch an updraft off the lake and soar over you. If it's fall, spend some time on the deck admiring the colors and laughing at the chipmunks scurrying for that last acorn. If winter cold has you down, take the time to sip a hot beverage while watching the bird feeders from your favorite chair. Marvel in the renewal of life in the spring—the flowers, the hummingbirds, the croaking frogs, before hitting the road.

You may still decide to call a Realtor or put a "For Sale By Owner" sign at the end of the driveway. That may be the best decision for you. Just don't expect me to follow suit. The bugs, birds, the damn tree-eating deer, and all my other neighbors had better get used to me. I'll be sticking around for a while.

Made in the USA
Middletown, DE
26 January 2017